Sib...

**Edited by
Stuart Hughes**

Hersham Horror Books

HERSHAM HORROR BOOKS
Logo by Daniel S Boucher

Cover Design by Mark West 2012

Copyright 2012 © Hersham Horror Books

ISBN: 978-1478320272

All rights belong to the original artists, and writers for their contributed works.

All rights reserved. No part of this book may be reproduced, scanned or distributed in any form, including digital and electronic or mechanical, including photocopying, recording, or by any information storage and retrieval system, without the prior written consent of the Publisher, except for brief quotes for use in reviews.

This book is a work of fiction. Characters, names, places and incidents either are the product of the author's imagination or are used fictitiously, and any resemblance to any actual persons, living or dead, events, or locales is entirely coincidental.

Pentanth No. 2

First Edition.

First published in 2012.

Contents

Foreword
Stuart Hughes
5

Chapter Bank
Simon Kurt Unsworth
7

Imogen
Sam Stone
27

Skin Deep
Richard Farren Barber
41

Always The Baby
Sara Jayne Townsend
69

My Little Sister
Stuart Hughes
91

Biographies
133

Also from
Hersham Horror Books:

Alt-Dead

Fogbound From 5

Alt-Zombie

Foreword

When Peter Mark May asked if I'd be interested in writing for and editing the second Hersham Horror PentAnth I naturally jumped at the chance. The first in the series, *Fogbound From 5*, was a fantastic read and would be a tough act to follow.

The first challenge was to pitch Peter an idea. I had a few ideas in mind, but uppermost at the time was a story idea I was wrestling with, featuring a male protagonist and his little sister. I had a vivid image in my mind that would ultimately become the story's denouement, but no understanding of how the protagonist would get there.

So I pitched the idea of *Siblings – five stories featuring brothers and sisters where at least one of the siblings had a dark secret.* An interesting idea, given I'm an only child. Peter went for it and the concept for the second Hersham Horror PentAnth was born.

Next I needed a cast of authors. I'm delighted to say that fortune smiled on me and I got the line-up I'd been hoping for. I am proud to be published in *Siblings* alongside the brilliant Simon Kurt Unsworth, Sam Stone, Richard Farren Barber and Sara Jayne Townsend.

The five stories in *Siblings* are very different in many ways. Each author brings their own voice and style to the story telling process and you won't be disappointed. There's supernatural horror between these pages, psychological horror, not to a mention a monster or two.

Stuart Hughes
Derbyshire
July 2012

Hersham Horror Books

Siblings

Chapter Bank

Simon Kurt Unsworth

"Can you come?"

Hollister's midnight brain didn't move as quickly as his mouth and he was still trying to work out who the voice at the end of the line belonged to as he said, "Hey, Sis."

"Can you come?" Bex said again and then her voice hitched itself down into tears. Hollister lay in his half-asleep, half-empty bed listening to her, wondering how long it was since they had last spoken. Eighteen months? Twenty four? Longer, thirty six at least; before he and Dee married, certainly. He shouldn't get involved, he knew. This was Bex's pattern, the big explosion over nothing, the long sulk and the silence and then the dramatic return begging for help, and it never ended well for anyone. He'd had it all his life, all of them had, he and Dad and Mum, and it was exhausting. Little Bex, so fragile and mercurial, so pretty and aware of her own prettiness, so helpless.

Whatever this was, he should say no, should disconnect the call and roll over, go back to sleep. He looked over at the empty half of his bed, the sheets rumpled and shadowed and cold, and did not move the phone from his ear.

"Please, Richard," Bex said, her voice sounding distant and lost, reaching out to him from every Christmas and Birthday of childhood, from every Sunday meal and summer holiday, from every argument and every good time, taking hold of him and *pulling*, just like it always had. "Please, Richard, he's following me and I can't stop him. I'm frightened, Richard, so frightened, please come, please help me."

"Where are you?" he asked, sighing.

"I'm at home," she said, her voice echoing in the space between them.

"I'll come tomorrow," he said and it was only after he put the phone down that the reality of it came, hard and raw and cold and crashing him into wakefulness; Bex was dead, and had been for nearly three months.

The next morning's light was bright enough to make Bex's call seem dreamlike and thin, something half-imagined and not entirely real, and Hollister wondered what he should do. He couldn't pretend that nothing had happened, much as he might want to; either he had imagined it, in which case he had to assume it was his unconscious telling him he was ready to deal with his younger sister's death in some way, or she had rung him from some place he didn't want to contemplate because she needed help. Whichever it was, he supposed he would have to go. What else could he do? Whatever her faults, whatever the problem, she was his sister, and he would go to her because she asked. How could he not?

He was packed and on the road by ten, and arrived at lunchtime.

Chapter Bank was tiny, a cluster of houses and shops miles from the nearest town, lost to everything except itself at the end of a road that curled and twisted over the brows of hills and through the river-cut valleys. The last part of the journey, the road became a dark, single lane strip cut into the earth and Hollister wondered what might happen if he met something coming the other way as he drove, but he did not; there were no cars, no trucks or bikes, no people, just sheep grazing the grassland that hemmed around the road and a blue sky filled with cottony clouds above him.

How had she ended up here? Hollister wondered as he pulled into one of the parking spaces that lined Chapter Bank's small green? Bex, who hated the countryside and being bored, who liked lights and noise and things that glittered and sparkled, how had she come to this place? Why? After that last argument, when she had accused him and Dee of selfishness for wanting to marry and have children, why had she come here? She had lived like a recluse, he remembered the coroner saying, for the months before her death, rarely leaving her home, shopping online and having things delivered rather than going to the local shops. She had cut herself off from not just Hollister and Dee but from everyone, it seemed, existing in Chapter Bank for three years in a house bought with her part of their inheritance, and her death had been accidental, a fall down stairs whilst drinking that snapped her neck as cleanly as a piece of old wood broken for kindling. There were no suspicious circumstances, the police said, just another lonely person dying, found by the postman when he needed a signature for a parcel but couldn't get an answer at her front door and had peered in through the window.

Suddenly, Hollister was struck by a sense of loss and guilt so powerful that he felt faint, tears building behind his eyes, threatening to spill down his cheeks. How could he have lost contact with her so completely? Why hadn't he made an effort to find her? Because she and Dee didn't get on? Because life was quieter, easier without Bex in it? Because he was too wrapped up in his own grief over their parents' death? Because he was too lost in his own problems to think about anyone else's? All this and more, he thought, and now it was too late; Bex was gone, Dee was gone, his parents were gone and there was nothing he could do about any of it.

His mobile buzzed, distracting him from his thoughts. He pulled it from his pocket and put it to his ear, connecting to the call. "Are you coming?" asked Bex, her voice echoing, tearful. "Richard, are you coming? He's nearly caught me, Richard, he's so close."

"Bex?" he asked, his skin prickling. His mouth went dry, felt as cotton-filled as the clouds had looked. "Who's after you?"

"He is, Richard, the *boy*. The boy is coming," she said and then the call broke, wailing distortion before disconnecting completely. He held the phone away from his ear and then scrolled through its menu to the recent calls listings. The name at the top of the list simply read SIS. What would happen if he pushed the Call button, he wondered? Would she answer? Would someone else answer and reveal this to be some kind of elaborate, unpleasant joke? Would it simply ring and ring?

His thumb hovered and then fell away, not wanting to know. *I'm a coward,* he thought. He looked at the phone for a long time before putting it back in his pocket.

When Hollister got out of his car, he discovered that Chapter Bank smelled good, the air fresh and clean and thick with grass and birdsong. He started to walk, wanting to stretch his legs, and thinking that he and Dee might have liked it here. He passed its one pub and several small shops, a butcher's and a newsagent's, before coming to the edge of the green. At its centre was a war memorial, an old and black piece of statuary with names chiselled into its front. Across the base, he saw, someone had sprayed SHE WALKS in bright yellow paint. *Not only that,* he thought, *she calls as well,* and despite himself, despite the situation, he grinned.

It was time to go to her house.

He had assumed that finally entering Bex's home would give him some kind of answer, present a solution to him, but it did not.

The house was an old farmer's cottage situated at the end of a narrow track that his car jumped and jolted along, the police tape still fluttered from one of the gateposts slapping into his window as he passed it. There were bunches of flowers and wreaths scattered across the front garden and Hollister's car rolled over them as he parked. They stank of sweet decay when he opened the door, and slithered under his feet as he went to the door. Cards floated among the rotting leaves. He saw one that read, *We're so sorry*, and another, *Be at peace.*

Hollister picked this last one up. The card was sealed in a small plastic envelope, and it was clean, the bouquet it was attached to fresher, laid on top of one whose flowers were little more than black clenches of petals atop curling green stems.

This hasn't been here three months, Hollister thought. *A month at most, maybe less.*

Looking around, he saw other fresher bouquets amongst the older ones, as well as single flowers and one teddy bear, its fur bedraggled and faded. Looking back, he saw flowers had been tied to the stones along the top of the boundary wall and to the wooden struts of the opened gates; some were drooping and dead, others looked colourful, fresh. Dropping the card, he entered the house.

There were the remains of more flowers throughout the house, these in vases, and he thought that they were probably here from when Bex was alive. The house stank of them, and the first thing he did was to open all the windows and then find a refuse bag to put all the dead blooms in. He poured the stagnant water down the sink, running the water for a long time to clear it, and then threw most of the vases into the bag with the flowers, which he then sealed and placed outside.

By the time he had finished, Hollister had been in every room in what had been Bex's house; his house now, he supposed. It was small, two bedrooms and a bathroom over a kitchen, lounge and utility. He sat for a long time at the bottom of the stairs, in the place where Bex had died, trying to feel her, but felt nothing. She wasn't here, not now anyway.

There was old food in the kitchen, mostly packets and microwave meals that had gone out of date. Hollister threw it all away as well. The fridge was thankfully empty and disconnected from the wall. In the cupboard under the sink he found a mass of vodka and whisky bottles, some full but most empty. There was something sad about the dusty bottles, hidden away, and he felt like crying again. He opened one of the whisky bottles and sniffed at the peaty aroma that rose from it, debated taking a swig, and then replaced its top without doing so.

Bex's phone was by her bed, on a table that also held a glass from which the water had evaporated and left grey rings around its inner surface, and a strip of birth control pills. Four of the pills were gone and the phone held no charge. There were piles of paperwork in most of the rooms, unopened mail as well as bills and flyers and other documents. It was going to take him a few days to go through it all, he supposed, if he stayed here.

He thought again about the calls, about Bex's voice, and wondered why he wasn't scared. *Because, even if she's a ghost, she's my sister,* he thought. *What harm can she do me?*

He needed food if he was going to stay here. Hollister locked the house and went out into the warm air, treading warily over the carpet of flowers. They slithered under his feet, their scent rotten and thick, and he only saw the woman as he reached his car.

She was standing just inside the drive and he thought it was Bex at first, but she was older than Bex, somewhere in her sixties.

"Hello?" he said.

The woman dropped the bunch of flowers she was holding, the blooms scattering the ground around her, and turned, walking out of the gate and disappearing from his view. He went after her, calling again, but by the time he reached the road there was no sign of her. Crouching, he looked at the flowers she had dropped. The card tied around the stems read simply, *Rest peaceful.*

When Hollister looked up, Bex was standing in the doorway of the house.

She hadn't changed, not much. She was a little thinner, her hair longer and less styled than it used to be, tangled around her face in whorls and knots. She was holding her arms up, her hands open, reaching towards him, and she looked miserable. No, not miserable, *terrified*. She was speaking, her mouth mouthing, writhing, but he heard no sound.

"Bex?" he said, standing, absurdly aware of the sound of his knees popping and thinking, *I'm getting old.*

She didn't reply, not in words. Instead, she stepped towards him, her mouth still moving, chewing at words he could not hear. Behind her, lights began to show through the opaque quarter windows in the top of the front door. The light was bright, yellow, and as it fell on Bex's shoulders she flinched, hunching down as though it was burning her. She cast a glance back towards the door and then turned back towards Hollister, her face twisting, the bags under her eyes cast into black pools by the light.

"Bex," he said again and stepped towards her. His feet kicked aside petals and buds, the sound of them like silk slipping against silk. The light was building, growing brighter, glimmering not only in the windows of the door but also the other windows, as though the house itself was filling with it. It was brighter than the day around it, brighter than the sun above Hollister, and then Bex was gone, scurrying away from the door and collapsing to nothing as she passed through the shadows below one of the windows. The light was gone moments after she was.

It had been Bex, Hollister thought, *Bex. His sister. His baby sister, frightened and asking for help, and what was going on here? What?*

What?

"Have you come to take her away?" the man asked.

The drive back into Chapter Bank hadn't taken long, but Hollister felt as though he was being watched from behind every curtain and from every shadowed alleyway. People on the street turned to watch him as he rolled past and when he parked in one of the spaces along the side of the small square, he saw people standing looking at him from the other side of the grass. He raised his hand to them, but they did not respond.

Chapter Bank didn't have a supermarket, so Hollister went into the corner shop. It was cool inside, the heat kept at bay by a long, old-fashioned fridge that was full of meats and cheeses. He gathered an armful of food and placed it on the counter, following it with soft drinks and a couple of bottles of wine. It was as he was paying that the man behind the counter spoke.

"Pardon?" he asked, and then realised that the man was staring at the keys in his other hand; he had taken them out of his pocket to get to his wallet. No, he thought, the man wasn't staring at the keys, but at the address written on the brown card tag that dangled from them, attached by a piece of white cotton twine and spinning slowly. Bex's keys had been sent to Hollister as her only surviving relative, labelled by the police or the coroner or one of their solicitors, he supposed; she hadn't left a will and the only officials he had dealt with were the ones investigating her death.

"Her. The girl. Have you come to take her away?"

"I'm sorry," Hollister said again, "I don't understand."

"You have the keys to her house," said the shopkeeper, finally looking up and into Hollister's face. "She's here. She's always here. Every night."

"In the shop?" Hollister asked, aiming for a tone of voice somewhere between facetious and amused but suspecting he failed and came across as numb and slow.

"Everywhere," the man said simply. "All the village. Everyone sees her, and we all hear her. No one sleeps for long any more because she comes to us. Please, can you take her away?"

"I don't know," Hollister said, picking up his purchases. *Oh, Sis, what are you doing here*, he thought, suddenly angry. *Where are you?* What *are you?* As if in reply, his phone rang again, the sound of it shrill in the shop. Behind the counter, the old man backed away, leaving the money where Hollister had dropped it.

Hollister reached inside his pocket and removed the phone, holding it in the same hand as the keys.

"Hello?" he said after answering the call and the shopkeeper began to moan, backing further away and bumping into the shelves behind him.

"Hello?" Hollister said again but the only reply was the sound of someone weeping, the sobs echoing and swooping and repeating, as though he was hearing them from a great distance. He didn't look at the display to find out who was calling; he already knew.

"Please," said the shopkeeper. "Take her away. Please."

As he left the shop, Hollister lost his grip on his food and some of it fell. One of the bottles of wine smashed on the floor and sprayed his ankles with chardonnay, the smell of it sweet and sharp. He stumbled, leaving the mess for the man to clear up, and went out into the sunlight. He felt as though he'd fallen into some weird fever dream, something unreal and hallucinatory. He dropped more of the food as he got outside, bacon and bread falling from his arms in ungainly arcs. His vision had blurred, tears spilling from him, hot and scalding. The phone in his pocket rang again, and he slapped at it, hoping to turn it off through the cloth, dropping the last of his shopping. A bottle of cola bounced and rolled, coming to rest against the feet of the woman who was standing at the edge of the pavement.

She was at the head of a group of six or seven people, all of them motionless, watching him. Hollister straightened, wiping the tears from his face, trying to ignore his phone's shrill call.

"It's her," the woman said. It was the woman who had been at Bex's house a few minutes ago, he realised. Her hair was grey and her face square and set and she looked tired; they all did, this little crowd that had gathered around him, closing in, tightening like a human noose, driving him back against the wall. Some of them were older than the woman, some younger, their only apparent link the exhaustion that was painted across their faces, sagging skin and bruised flesh under their eyes. They gathered around him.

"I'm sorry, genuinely, but I don't understand," he said.

"It's her," the woman said, and gestured towards his pocket. The phone had stopped ringing and its silence was almost as heavy as its noise had been.

"I don't–" Hollister began again but the woman interrupted him fiercely.

"You do! It's her! She's still here, she won't go. She runs through the village every night, through our homes and our dreams, always calling, always crying, neverstopping. She's running from the light, desperate to avoid the inevitable, trying to hold on to something she's got no right to."

"No."

"Yes. You're her brother." It wasn't a question.

"Yes."

"You have to persuade her to go where she needs to go. She can't stay here, feeding on us. She liked flowers, so we take her flowers, but they don't satisfy her. You're blood, you can help her."

"No," but it was true, wasn't it? That was Bex all over, always running, always angry, never satisfied, turning her anger outwards and expecting people to simply carry it for her. He had a sudden image of her at the centre of a spreading pool of black, clinging liquid, staring at her house and gradually widening, covering the village, soaking everyone in it. A tendril had reached out to him because of a groove worn between him and Bex by their history, but how far could it reach eventually? How much sleep could she steal? How many dreams could she infect?

How many people could she hurt?

"I don't know what to do," he said.

"Love her," said the woman. "And persuade her to stop running."

Persuade her to stop running, Hollister thought when he arrived back at the house. *So easy to say, but how the fuck do I do it?* They didn't know Bex, didn't know the impossibility of changing her mind once it was set. If she had decided to run, to avoid the light, then she would run forever rather than change direction. She hadn't liked Dee, and nothing had changed her mind about that; hated it that he and Dee had talked about children, not because she thought that they would be bad parents but simply because she, Bex, didn't like children. Hollister had always denied it in the arguments with Dee, but suspected in his secret thoughts that Bex hated the idea of him and Dee starting a family so much because it would mean he wasn't as available for *her*.

My sister was selfish, he thought, the first time he had ever really allowed himself to think it. *Selfish, and shallow, and manipulative, but she was my sister and I loved her. I still love her.*

The evening was quiet. Bex didn't ring again and the thought that she was sulking because he hadn't answered her earlier calls, that she was a sulking ghost, made him smile, although it was a smile that felt weighted with tears.

He drank the wine that had survived his dropping it and ate some of the bread and bacon, chewing mechanically and not really tasting what he swallowed. He found the power cable for Bex's phone and charged it up, half wondering if he might be able to ring her on it, and then dismissed the idea; this would, as in everything else, be done to Bex's timetable. Instead, he read through some of the piles of paperwork, casting most of it into a bag for disposal.

Most were bills, their payment dates long gone, which he put on one side to see if they had been paid or not. There were leaflets and flyers, magazines still in their plastic sheaths about flower arranging and home making, brochures for local fast food delivery services, the detritus of months of deliveries. In one pile, he found a collection of letters tied together with a black ribbon; when he started to read them, he found that they were from a man he had never heard of. He stopped reading after looking over a couple of them because they were full of sexual innuendo and it felt as though he was snooping, opening up something private that he felt should remain closed.

At some time around midnight, Hollister went into the kitchen to get himself a glass of water before sleep.

Peering at the reflection of his face in the window over the sink, he saw himself pale and thin, his eyes droplets of ink on alabaster skin. *Here I am again,* he thought and then saw the glow in the garden.

There was a light coming from the far end of the grass, fracturing apart his reflection, washing out his face and replacing it with the gaunt outlines of tangled grass and plants left to grow without attention. The glow filled the space in front of his eyes, brighter and bright, fingers of light reaching out to him. Hollister pressed his face against the glass, cupping his hands around his eyes to try and see more clearly, but had to turn away because of the intensity of it. In the moment before he turned away, there seemed to be a figure at the centre of the glare, tiny and dark and moving forwards. He turned, expecting to see Bex, or to hear his phone ring, but there was nothing, and when he looked back, both the light and the figure had vanished.

Hollister didn't fall asleep but lay on the bed in Bex's room thinking. It was a cliché, wasn't it? Dead people and bright lights? But just because it was a cliché didn't mean there wasn't some truth there, surely?

Was Bex avoiding the light? Clinging to life, reaching out in dreams and through his phone, desperately trying to hold on to him, to someone, to something so that she wouldn't be dead? He could imagine her doing that, refusing to accept her situation, fighting it, making everyone else suffer just to help her achieve what she wanted, no matter how impossible. And where did that leave him? There was no way he could change things, he didn't think; he had never been able to change her mind about anything when she was alive, so why should things be different when she was dead?

Hollister wondered why it mattered to him, to get Bex to go into the light. For her good? Maybe. To know he had helped her do this last thing? Maybe. She was his sister and he cared about her, yes, but he was, if he was honest, angry at her. She had placed strains on him and Dee that they had not survived, caused his parents all sorts of stresses and miseries, and yet always seemed to emerge from these situations as though nothing had happened; perhaps, now he had a chance, a final chance, to give his sister the kind of peace she had constantly refused herself in life. She had set herself against the light, and would stay set against it as long as she could, which left only one option as far as he could see.

He would have to trick her.

The screaming started at thirteen minutes past two.

It was coming from downstairs, ragged whoops and cries of pain and terror. Hollister thought he recognized Bex's voice in the screams but couldn't be sure, so ragged where they. He looked at his watch, remembering what the coroner's report had said; that Bex had been dead for perhaps six or seven hours when the postman found her at almost nine in the morning. Was this her death he was listening to? Some nightly recreation of her last moments? He went to the bedroom door, listening. The screams continued, hoarse, wordless.

I am not afraid, he told himself, *because she is my sister*. Then, taking a deep breath, he stepped out and looked down the stairs.

There was nothing there.

What had he expected? he wondered as another scream tore the air? The spectral image of his dying sister? Bex shrieking and glimmering and holding out her hands, a ghost on the phone. Perhaps she could text him, *Dear Bro I'm Dead Help me Thnx.*

I'm going mad, he thought, and started down the stairs. He was halfway down when his phone rang. The noise, so normal, sounded shrill in the night-time darkness of the house, its forced jollity jolting Hollister, making him jump. He fumbled it from his pocket, looking at the display. It read simply, SIS. He looked back up at the house's upper floor, knowing that Bex's phone was in the bedroom he had just come from. His phone rang again and he pressed the button to connect to the call.

"Richard, are you there?" Bex said.

"I'm here," he said, and she sounded so scared, so distant, her voice echoing and repeating, that he sat down, his legs suddenly nerveless and weak. Light was beginning to bleed out form under the kitchen door, spreading in pallid streaks across the floor.

"He's coming, Richard," Bex said. "He nearly caught me but I hid, but he keeps finding me."

"Who?"

"The boy," she said.

"Come to me, Bex," said Hollister. He used the bannister to stand, keeping the phone by his ear, watching the kitchen door. The light was growing brighter, strips of it growing up along the jambs, the edge of the hinges silhouetted, casting angular shadows. The door began to open, more light falling out.

"Bex?" Hollister said and then she was in front of him, stepping out across the hallway towards him. The light was tautening, brightening, filling the doorway behind her. She looked back over her shoulder, her face drawn, her mouth twisting down. Her arms were out towards

Hollister, her hands empty, and her voice crackled in his phone again, "Richard, help me."

"I will, Bex," he said. "Look at me, just look at me."

She looked back around, peering at Hollister. Her face was pale, her skin the colour of whey, her legs and hands streaked with darkness. In the light behind her, a black shape was coalescing, thickening just above the floor. Bex moaned as though she could feel it and Hollister said again, "Look at me, Sis, just keep looking at me. It'll be okay Sis, there's no need to be frightened."

The light carried on expanding, filling the hallway, blurring Bex's edges as she moaned again. Hollister could see nothing past Bex now, the kitchen doorway and the room beyond lost to the brightness. The black mark in the light's centre was growing, resolving itself into the shape of a child standing behind Bex with its arms outstretched.

"Richard!" she cried and stepped towards him.

"Stay still, Bex. Stay still and stop running. You don't belong here, you belong there." Hollister was crying now, seeing his sister properly for the first time in three years, remembering her face and her laugh, remembering the tiny kindness she sometimes committed, the time she had turned up with a bottle of whisky for him, the time she had called him and made him laugh telling him filthy jokes.

"Richard," she said again and the child behind her moved closer, the light knitted together into the shape of a boy, a toddler who was naked and chubby. His hands, fingers opening and closing, fastened on to her leg and she shrieked, kicking back.

"Don't be frightened," Hollister said. "Go into the light, Sis, go with it. Let it take you where you need to be. I love you, Rebecca," and he was no longer crying, he was weeping, tears falling from his cheeks, slicking the hand holding the phone, and his voice was thick and near-unintelligible.

Bex shrieked and the child pulled at her, tugging her back inexorably towards the doorway. The light flared more brightly, dissolving the two figures in the hallway into little more than wavering shadows, printing afterimage puppets across Hollister's eyelids. The phone in his hand, always Bex's preferred method of communication, wailed, the noise wavering and then dwindling forlornly. For a moment, Bex surged out of the light towards him, her hands out and her mouth open wide. One last, wrenching cry came from the phone and now it was coming from Bex as well, piercingly loud, full of anger and fear and then it, too, collapsed and she was gone, slipping back into the glare.

"I love you," Hollister said, and dropped the now-silent phone to the floor.

Ahead of him, the light folded in on itself, circling around to nothing, leaving only streaked shadows in its wake. The house settled and then relaxed, and only his tears remained

"I love you," he said for a third time, and then, "Rest easy, Sis."

He thought that would be the end of it, but it wasn't.

There was something wrong, he thought, something that didn't fit. He had done what was needed, the last thing he could do for her, helping her to accept and go into the light. Hadn't he? Only, he told himself later, sitting at the kitchen table with a coffee and peering into the garden as dawn crept across the edges of the world, she had never accepted it, not even right at the end when she was already within the light. She had fought and fought against it, clinging on as tightly as she could to whatever kind of existence she could grasp, but why? Why was she so determined to avoid the light?

Unless it wasn't the light she had been avoiding, but the thing the light contained; unless she was avoiding the child. 'The boy', she had kept saying, she was avoiding *the boy*.

Why should Bex be frightened of a child? Hollister wondered and then thought, as the world pitched beneath his feet, that he might know.

He retrieved the letters from the pile in the lounge and flicked through them; the last, dated not long after Bex moved to Chapter Bank, was brusque, saying simply that if Bex refused to reply to letters or calls then the writer could only assume she no longer wanted to see him. He thought of the screams and gasps he had heard from the kitchen, the crying, and imagined blood lying across the cheap tiled floor, and sweat and pain and fear.

Hollister walked out into the garden. In the pre-dawn light, the air was chill and raised gooseflesh across his arms. The light he had seen through the window had been coming from the far border, he remembered, and it didn't take him long to dig down and find the bones. He wanted to believe the child had been born dead, but he knew it hadn't. It had been born alive and buried holding its arms out for its mother, and his sister had spent the next years hiding and running and pretending that the world outside the walls of her home didn't exist.

Bex's dead child had come for her, born by light, and Hollister had forced her into its arms and told her he loved her even as she burned in the child's embrace.

He sat in the garden and wept, brushing dirt from the tiny bones, and all around him the light of a world that would never be bright again filled the sky.

Imogen

Sam Stone

Imogen had been blatant that night. She wanted Michael to know how she felt, wanted to share her love, her sex, her emotions, before they bubbled out unchecked for everyone to see. Day after day she was holding it together but the nights were the worst. She wanted him even though she knew it was a sin and no number of Hail Marys was ever going to change that.

Imogen sat in the dark waiting for Michael to return. It was late. He was often home by two, but that night he still hadn't arrived by four. She was worried. She rubbed her eyes, reached for the cold cup of coffee beside her chair and glanced down at the bare flesh that showed through the slit in her nightdress. Her hand slid over her thigh and her fingers slipped under the fabric until they stroked the bare skin there. She imagined it was *his* hand, skin slightly roughened from his job as a carpenter, that touched the intimate and soft area between her legs.

At some point in the night she had dozed in the chair. It helped to ease the long hours, and it meant she didn't see the painful bleakness of dawn struggling through the wintery clouds. Sleeping on the job, so they say, was a dangerous game she sometimes played. What would he think if he came home and found her in *his* chair, with so little clothing on? Nothing probably. That was the thing: he wouldn't even notice. All he saw when he looked at her was his little sister. But then, how could she possibly expect him to think of her in any other way?

Imogen stood and stretched, the thin shoulder strap of her nightdress fell and the fabric slipped down, revealing one of her pert small breasts. She looked down at it. If only Michael would come home now. She was so ready to show him how she felt. Her hand slipped over the fabric, briefly cupped her breast and then she pulled up the strap, covering herself.

Headlights illuminated the room as a car pulled into the drive and Imogen's heart jumped in her chest. Her resolve diminished instantly and she ran for the stairs taking them two at a time. At the top she glanced back down before turning and heading straight to her room at the front of the house. She didn't look out as the engine switched off, but instead slipped into her bed and lay there, heart pounding.

She heard the front door open: although as always, Michael was trying to be quiet. A dull scraping noise told her that the chain was now in place. She lay in the bed, her legs apart, hoping he would come in, but knowing he wouldn't. For a while longer she could make out the muted sounds of Michael moving around the house.

Work clothing in the washing machine, she thought. *Glass of juice from the fridge.*

Imogen knew her brother's routine so well she barely heard the noises but recognised them anyway. Michael was very fastidious about hygiene. He would be in the bathroom shortly brushing his teeth. *There.* Water ran into the sink. The shower switched on.

Oh Michael. She imagined his rough hands running over his own body, washing away the day's grime. She imagined him naked and hard and eager.

The shower switched off. Imogen's hand rested on her pubis as she listened. Then she heard Michael open his bedroom door. It wasn't long before his soft snores filtered through the wall.

She brought herself to a guilty orgasm. Then lay panting softly. Wishing again that she wasn't his sister. It all seemed so unfair.

In the morning she ate breakfast alone, Michael was still in bed. She hated the late shifts he worked. They barely spent any time together at all. Since their mother died, Michael had taken extra hours, worked harder, all in the name of supporting them both.

At lunchtime Imogen heard the shower again and soon Michael came downstairs.

"Hi," she said.

"Morning."

Michael looked tired but relaxed. His blond hair was washed and combed back wet from his face. His blue eyes were bright as he smiled at her. His colouring was so different from hers. Imogen brushed back her dark hair and scrutinised Michael with her hazel eyes. Sometimes she daydreamed that they weren't related at all. Their colouring was so different that this wasn't so hard to imagine. They were in fact opposites.

"How was your day, Gen?" he asked.

"A little dull. I missed you."

Michael nodded his head but said nothing as he sat down at the kitchen table. Imogen put a cup of coffee – white, two sugars, just as he liked it – down on the table before him. Then she sat down opposite him.

"I thought I might go down to the job centre today," Imogen said. "It's not fair that you have to work so hard all the time when I'm more than cap-"

"No," Michael said firmly. "You need to stay home, Gen. *That's* your job."

Imogen felt that knot of anxiety she sometimes felt when she wanted to disagree with Michael. He was pretty stubborn. He took after their mother that way. His ego would cause him no end of trouble one day, but it was impossible to argue with him.

Michael placed his hand on hers and looked at her over the table.

"I promised Mum that I'd look after you. And I will. Always."

Imogen's face lit up as Michael looked into her eyes, but her brother suddenly blushed and pulled back his hand.

The guilt came again. She shouldn't love him this way. She had to be careful. Surely he knew how she felt? She couldn't help reading into his reaction though, always giving herself false hope. *What if the blush means he feels the same?*

Imogen stood up and went to the dishwasher. Her hands were trembling, her heart pounding in her chest. All the thoughts and feelings she carried inside her rumbled around and yelled "sinner" inside her head. She began to fill the machine with the breakfast dishes and dirty mugs, but her fingers were clumsy and one of the glasses fell from her hand and smashed down on the tiled floor.

"What the fuck …?"

Michael stood but Imogen was already cleaning up the mess. She knew how he hated chaos. She had to keep the house clean for him. *That* was her job.

"Mind you don't cut your–" Michael said calmly.

"It's fine. I'm fine," she answered. "Sorry."

She made him chicken salad for lunch. He ate it silently while sipping orange juice.

"Must get back to work," he said pushing back his chair. "Cupboards don't build themselves."

Imogen said nothing but watched him pick up his tool bag. Inside she knew were all the things he needed to work. She remembered watching him build a cupboard recently. It might even have been a wardrobe. He had caressed the wood, smoothed and shaped it: worked with so much love and care that she couldn't help admiring his hands as they moved. Perhaps that was even the moment when she realised she loved him more than she should.

"Will you be late tonight?" she asked as he pulled his jacket from the coat rack by the door.

"No. This job is almost finished. Should be back early. About six."

"I'll make dinner then," Imogen said.

After he left, the house felt empty. Imogen cleaned and tidied and emptied the washing machine. She shook out Michael's overalls and examined the stains. Brown smears marred the cloth. Imogen knew it was wood stain but the splatter made her feel uneasy. It never came out fully, and to Michael it probably didn't matter at all. After all next time he wore them more stain would find its way onto the cloth. Imogen wanted them cleaner though and so she put the wash back on and ran the cycle twice more before switching the load over to the drier.

Then she chopped some vegetables and made a beef casserole.

"Gen? Are you home?"

Imogen jerked awake. She had dozed off in the chair in the lounge again and the hours had passed as though she didn't exist. There had been no dream but the sleep had been deep and sound.

"Must have fallen asleep," she said as Michael entered the room.

His eyes skittered over her and Imogen realised that she was still in her night clothes and her robe was lying open exposing her leg.

"It's six," he said.

"Oh good. Dinner should be perfect now."

They went into the kitchen and Michael sat once more at the table as Imogen passed him a bowl and a plate with a crusty roll on. Then she placed a bottle of red wine and two glasses down. They sat together talking about the day, but Imogen could barely make conversation as hers had been so dull. She listened to Michael talk though. He loved his work and his affinity with his craft was evident in his words.

"I might have to go out again tonight," Michael said. "There is one last thing that needs to be finished on this job and there seems little point in leaving it undone when it would only take me an hour or so."

"Oh that's a shame. I thought we would watch something on TV together. Michael I hardly see you. I'm alone so much."

Michael looked down at his plate and took a sharp breath. He seemed on the verge of saying something but instead he stood up, bumped the table and knocked his glass over. The wine splashed over the table and onto Imogen's robe. She looked down, watched the wine seep into the cloth like a blood stain on her abdomen.

Michael stared at her, then backed away.

"I can't do this Gen. Not again!"

Imogen heard the front door slam and she stared at the spilt wine and the stain and her empty bowl. Nothing made sense. She had upset him, but didn't know how. She removed the robe and placed it in the washer.

At two she heard him return. She waited downstairs as always, saw the headlights, hurried to her room. It was a cycle that repeated night after night. Sometimes she lingered outside his door while he slept. She knew that entering his room would be bad but she couldn't help toying with the idea. She would pace silently, waiting for him to wake and find her there. She wished again and again that they weren't related. That she was just some girl that lived in the same house as him. Not his sister, but his lover.

It was as though she only lived when he came home. Each day was the same. She cooked, she cleaned, she washed his overalls, and then he would return and fall asleep leaving her lonely.

"Something weird happened today," she said. "I waved at the neighbour when she was in her garden. She was looking straight at me but completely ignored me. She used to be so friendly. I think I must have upset her somehow?"

"I'll speak to her," Michael said.

"It was odd, wasn't it?"

"Yes."

"If I have offended her, will you apologise? I didn't mean it. But I might have said something without realising."

"I'm sure it's nothing …"

That night Michael didn't go out. They sat watching the television and he nursed the remote control as he always did. Imogen didn't mind. She felt alive and calm and happy. She always felt more vital when Michael was around.

At bedtime she followed him upstairs. She waited while he used the bathroom, then stood awkwardly at the top of the stairs as he opened his bedroom door.

"Michael?"

"I'm tired, Imogen."

"Can I …?"

"Good night," he said closing his door firmly shut.

Imogen jumped awake as she heard the phone ringing beside her. She had fallen asleep in the chair again. Her hand took the receiver and she pressed it against her ear before she realised that Michael had already answered.

"Good morning gorgeous," said a female voice. "I missed you last night."

Imogen was too surprised to speak.

"Stacey …" Michael's voice sounded sleepy and soft.

"So … I was thinking I might come over to your place tonight instead."

"No. I'll come to you. Things are a bit messy here at the moment."

Imogen listened as Michael talked about the chaos at home. She looked around the immaculate lounge and wondered what it was that she wasn't doing properly. She placed the receiver down quietly as Michael finished his conversation, and then she sneaked upstairs and back into her room before he discovered that she was awake.

She felt hurt that he hadn't mentioned his new girlfriend and that he had lied to her about where he was all of those evenings. Clearly he wasn't working so late all the time. He was sleeping with his new whore instead.

Imogen felt a terrible rage. Her ears burst with noise as her heart leapt in her chest. *There was someone else!* But then, what did she expect? She couldn't have him. Ever. She had to accept that and move on.

"Michael, why didn't you tell me you had a girlfriend?" she asked as she poured tea from the pot into his cup.

"What?"

"I heard you talking to her. Stacey, isn't it?"

Michael flushed with guilt.

"Gen, we've been through this before. I don't like to talk about these things with you."

"Why?"

"Because … because you don't take it well. But there's nothing to fear. I will look after you. Like I promised."

"I'm lonely. I'd like a boyfriend."

"Don't Imogen," Michael warned. His face was flushed and he appeared on the edge of anger.

"Maybe I'll go out today and find myself someone. Bring him back here and fuck him. How about *that*, Michael?"

"Stop it, Imogen. You know I don't like you to talk that way," Michael was so angry now, he gripped the table. "I won't hear any more about this. I'm entitled to have some life."

Imogen was angry too and she was suddenly not afraid to show it.

"I want a life too. I'm entitled to have life and love and sex, just the same as anyone else is."

Michael jumped up throwing his chair back. "You want sex do you? You dirty little whore. You want to tempt me again and again. Don't you remember where that led last time?"

He brought his open palm down across her face, hard, and the stinging slap rang through the kitchen and echoed out into the hallway.

Imogen fell against the sink but Michael wouldn't leave it there. She hadn't been chastised enough. He grabbed her hair, pulling her backwards until she fell down at his feet. He pulled open her robe, ripping at the nightdress.

"You fucking slut. Always lying around half dressed, always flaunting yourself. What do you expect me to do?"

Imogen felt his carpenter's hands roughly squeezing her bare breasts. But it wasn't sensual, or nice. Not at all as she had hoped. It hurt and she was scared.

"Do you know how hard it's been for me? Ever since that day? And it's all your fault, Imogen. All because you found those papers …"

Imogen couldn't understand what he was saying, she could feel his hands on her, and that was all that mattered. Even though there was no love in his touch at all. Everything that happened had been leading to this moment. She wanted him, was he finally taking care of everything?

She felt the knife penetrate her stomach and when she coughed, a gout of blood gushed from her mouth. But Michael didn't stop. He plunged the knife into her over and over again, like a parody of the sex act that could never happen between them.

"It's a sin. You dirty fucking tramp. Even if mother did adopt you. So what if we aren't really brother and sister? We were brought up that way and I can't want you. You're better off dead."

Blood poured on the floor. Something she would have to clean up when Michael had finished murdering her.

She lay still while he enjoyed himself: twisting and turning the knife while the red stuff spread over them both. His overalls were covered in stains by the time he discarded them, pushing them straight into the washing machine. The walls and cupboards were splattered in her blood.

"Get up," he said finally. "Clean this mess you made."

Imogen grimaced and pushed her intestines back inside her stomach. The hole closed. She staggered to her feet, sore and barely able to stand but still she hobbled over to the cupboard to find the mop and bucket. Then she cleaned up the blood while Michael sat at the table with a fresh pot of tea.

"I'm going out," he said.

"Will you be late?" she asked.

"Yes. Don't wait up for me."

Imogen slipped into oblivion again for a few hours. When she woke she found herself sitting once more in the chair. Her eyes were stinging. She sat in the dark waiting for Michael to return. It was late and she couldn't remember how she got there.

Her robe lay over the back of the chair and she was wearing her favourite nightdress. It was made of a pure white satin. She glanced down at her bare thigh and then back at the window. She was waiting for Michael. She was always waiting for Michael.

A car turned into the street and for a moment the headlights lit up the room. Imogen ran upstairs and went into her room. She lay down pulling the sheet over her.

Michael woke. He pushed aside the covers and sat up. The room was in darkness, but he could see the light peeking around the corners of the curtain. He smelt frying bacon, heard the kettle boil, and knew his sister would be making breakfast.

He shook away the horrible dream that still lurked in the back of his head. Imogen. A knife. Blood. It was all too awful to even consider.

He showered, washed his hair, and combed it back and away from his face. Then he shaved away the bristle. When he came out of the bathroom, he glanced at Imogen's room. The door was closed and he didn't like to go in, but she had left her robe over the edge of the bath.

He quietly entered her room and placed the robe on the chair at the bottom of the coffin. Then glanced through the glass panel to see the rotting face of his sister looking dispassionately back at him. His hand stroked the smooth lid of the coffin. It had been his finest work and no one but he would ever see it.

Downstairs Imogen placed a cup of coffee before him. Then a plate containing eggs and bacon, with toast that was slightly burnt.

She was wearing her favourite nightdress just to taunt him, but Michael chose to ignore it. Today he would be kind. Today he would pretend nothing was wrong. He hated to argue with her. Today things would end differently.

Michael sat and began to eat his breakfast.

Imogen sat opposite. The strap of her nightgown had fallen off one shoulder and she was wearing red lipstick. He could see her pale pink nipples showing through the sheer satin fabric.

"I thought I might look for work," she said. "It's not fair that you have to work so hard to support us."

"No," he said a little too sharply. "I promised Mum I'd look after you."

"Michael I found something today. Haven't you ever wondered why we look so different?"

"Don't, Gen. Let's not do this …" he pleaded. His stomach heaved against the bacon.

"We're not related. I was adopted," Imogen said.

Michael turned away as she slipped the nightdress down revealing her breasts.

"I'm not your sister."

"Stop it. I don't want to do this."

The satin fabric fell to the ground. Imogen was naked underneath and he could see the pink nipples that haunted his dreams and the fine black down between her legs.

"What are you?" he cried dropping his face into his hands. "Damn you. Can't you leave me alone?"

"I love you, Michael. I want to be your wife."

Michael felt Imogen's hand stroke his hair. He wanted to die but didn't feel brave enough to take his life.

"I'm sorry. I'm sorry. I didn't mean to hurt you."

"Death do us part," she said.

"You're dead … Can't you leave me in peace?"

"I want to be yours, Michael. Can't you see that?" Imogen smiled. "This time I'm giving you permission."

Michael pushed away from the table and backed up to the door but Imogen came forward holding out the knife.

"Kill me, Michael. Make me yours."

Michael took the knife. Maybe this time she would stay dead. He slashed and stabbed, twisted and turned. Blood covered the floor, the cupboards, the walls. Imogen was still. Then she turned her head and met his gaze with that cold, dead smile pasted on her painted lips.

"I had better clean up this mess," she said.

Michael stood. Removed his overalls and placed them in the washer.

Then he cried.

Skin Deep

Richard Farren Barber

Jonathan scrambled to answer the phone but Lydia was already awake. Her voice rose through the darkness, muffled by the bedding and a layer of sleep. "I thought you said the locums were on call tonight."

"They are."

"If they've got it wrong again then you need to have words." Her voice was shrill and he put a hand over the telephone to try and dampen the ring.

"I'll take it downstairs."

"Too late, I'm awake," his wife said. But he heard the bed springs creak as she rolled over on her side and he guessed that despite her protests she'd be asleep again inside ten minutes. He checked the alarm clock on his side of the bed – an instinct ingrained in him over the years of late night call-outs. Nearly three in the morning. Jonathan shuffled into his dressing gown as he navigated through the gloom and out into the corridor, and once the door was closed behind him he dared to press *answer*.

"Johnnie?"

He recognised his brother's voice and although he hated himself for it, Jonathan felt a pang of alarm.

"Tony?"

"Who else?" His brother laughed down the line. It was an embarrassed laugh that suggested that he understood that calling at three in the morning wasn't the right thing to do and, equally, he appreciated he had form. "I need you."

Three words. Jonathan felt chilled wind pressing against his shins below the dressing gown. He sat down on the top step of the staircase and held the phone to his ear, ready for whatever Tony had to tell him this time.

"What is it?"

"I'm sorry, I know I'm a crap brother, but this time I really need you."

"Can't we do this in the morning, like normal people?"

"Can you get over here?"

"Now?"

"And bring your Livingstone bag."

Jonathan smiled at the childhood reference – as soon as he put anything remotely medical inside a case Tony magically transformed it into a Livingstone bag.

"Are you all right?"

"No."

"What's wrong?"

Silence. And the silence caused the level of fear inside Jonathan to rise up another notch. The long, drawn out nothingness before Tony replied allowed Jonathan time to imagine all manner of disaster.

"Just get here as soon as you can. And bring the bag."

"Are you hurt? Have you called for an ambulance?"

That laugh again. Jonathan wanted to tell Tony to knock it off – they weren't kids any more and he was scaring him. But although Tony could be a prick, he didn't make calls on a whim.

"It'll take me about fifteen minutes to get there. Will you be all right?"

"I'll have to be."

Jonathan held the phone in his hand. It took him a moment to realise his brother had cut the line. He hurried back to the bedroom.

"What's baby brother done this time?"

"I thought you were asleep." He saw Lydia's outline rise up from the bed. She reached out and turned on the light. For a few seconds Jonathan couldn't see anything other than the flash of white.

"Sorry."

"It's not your fault you've got a loser for a brother." Her voice softened, but Jonathan realised that was only because she had someone other than him to blame for her disturbed night.

"He isn't a loser," he said automatically.

"No," Lydia said, but sarcasm infected her voice. "So why's he ringing now? To reminisce about his first day in primary school?"

"I need to go and see him."

Lydia blinked. "Now?" She sat up straighter and although he was ashamed, Jonathan took a little pleasure at her surprise – it wasn't just in her eyes, it rinsed through her whole body. "What's happened?"

"I don't know."

He pulled on his trousers and shirt from where he had dumped them by the side of the bed. As he dressed he made a mental checklist of what was in his bag downstairs. He didn't know what was wrong with Tony, and knowing Tony the possibilities were limitless, but he thought he had most eventualities covered.

"If he's been out thieving again–"

"He told me he'd stopped."

"And you believed him?"

Jonathan didn't answer; he didn't have time for this argument. In his head he was running through different scenarios. Had Tony ripped his leg open on a length of barbed wire? Been bitten by a security dog? Given the company Tony kept, a knife wound was possible. God, perhaps it was a gunshot? But surely even Tony wouldn't be stupid enough to think that his older brother could just drift in and sort him out if he'd been involved in a modern day recreation of the OK Corral.

"Don't let him get you mixed up in anything," Lydia said.

Jonathan looked across the room at his wife but didn't answer. *I already am*, he thought. *I have been since the moment he was born.*

"I've got my phone," he told her as he left the room. "I'll be back as soon as I can."

He ran down the stairs, fear rising almost as soon as he walked out of the light. His bag was in its niche by the door and he picked it up before reaching for the keys. The weight of the bag offered him some comfort; even if Tony had an inflated belief in the medical miracles he thought Jonathan could perform.

He shut the door behind him and strode out into the darkness, ready for whatever Tony had for him this time.

His younger brother lived in a house on the other side of town. The streets around him were littered with glass and old cars, and most of the windows on his road had at least one glass pane with a crack fixed by a length of brown masking tape. Jonathan had been over a few times, more often than he had admitted to Lydia, but still nowhere near as frequently as he ought to.

He parked the BMW outside Tony's house. It was the newest car on the road by far; the only one that looked like it could be expected to start on the first turn of the ignition key.

Tony's house was set apart from the terraces along the road – a grand Victorian structure that was slowly crumbling into the ground. Even now, Jonathan didn't really understand how his brother had come by the place; he knew there was something underhand about the deal – a win in a poker game most likely – but Jonathan chose not to ask too many questions. Over the years he'd realised that ignorance was usually the best way to cope with Tony.

At night the building took on the atmosphere of a classic haunted house – draped in deep shadows and lit only by a weak yellow bulb in one of the downstairs rooms. Jonathan sorted through his key ring until he found the Yale that Lydia didn't even know he possessed.

Jonathan knocked gently on the door and, when there was no immediate response, he used the key. The bottom of the door scraped against the floor inside the hallway; Tony's DIY skills to the fore.

"Tone?" Jonathan called out. His voice faded into the darkness. "Hey Tony, you here?"

No answer. Jonathan pulled the door closed behind him.

The hallway was filled with junk – the rusting frame of a bicycle, random shoes and boots, most of them encrusted in thick mud; a plastic bag full of old newspapers; and what looked like an old coal sack rammed with clothes. Jonathan hardly paused as he passed the collection.

He hurried toward the single light. The kitchen. He'd sat on rickety chairs in that room and talked for hour after hour with Tony – sometimes about inconsequential things like how crap the economy was or whether Forest would *ever* beat Derby, and sometimes deep and rambling drink-fuelled confessions from Tony about how he'd messed up his life or chapter and verse on his latest failed relationship. Jonathan loathed the room; it felt like every bad memory he had of Tony could be traced back to the kitchen of this house. This was where they'd been sitting when he had told his brother that their dad had Alzheimer's. This is where Tony had confessed his drug addiction for the first time. Where he had confessed almost everything.

Jonathan hated the yellow walls and the crumbling plaster. He hated the constant smell of gas from the leaky cooker and the taste of damp at the back of his throat that seemed to seep up through the floorboards from the cellar. The house wasn't haunted, but sometimes Jonathan felt that the kitchen was.

He took a deep breath and seized the handle. He had time enough to think to himself, *What is it this time?* before he pushed open the door.

"Jesus," he shouted. He rushed across the floor and dropped his bag beside his brother's body.

Tony was lying on the kitchen floor, a pool of blood spreading around his body. He had his eyes closed and Jonathan's first thought – clear as a loudspeaker – was, *He's dead, it's finally happened and he's dead*. He was wearing heavy welder's gloves and lying beside his body was a pair of thick rubber trousers. Streaks of blood, old mixed with new, ran across his face.

He opened his eyes and Jonathan felt relief swell in his chest.

Tony smiled, although it was hard for Jonathan to be certain. "Livingstone, I presume?"

"Gladstone," Jonathan muttered. "It's a Gladstone bag." He laid his hands on his brother's chest, lightly, ever so lightly, and yet Tony still hissed at the contact.

"What the fuck happened? It looks like you've done ten rounds with Carl Froch and a baseball bat."

He tried to take in the scene calmly, but he was more conscious than he had ever been in his life that he was no paramedic, just a GP.

Just a GP, his mind rang crazily. He looked down at the broken mess of his brother's body and that phrase clanged in his mind like an alarm bell, *just a GP*. He pulled out his phone. "We need an ambulance."

"No." Tony reached out his hand to stop him, although he didn't have the strength to do so. For a second Jonathan thought he saw the skin of his brother's hand flex, as if something had moved beneath it. Just for a second.

"I can't do this."

Tony smiled. "Yes you can, Bro. You can do anything."

Jonathan felt the muscles in his chest tighten at the misplaced confidence. Maybe it wasn't as bad as it seemed, and Tony would no doubt have a very good reason for not wanting this to appear on any official records.

Jonathan opened his case and took out a scalpel.

"Hold on," Tony said. His words slurred and Jonathan tried not to think what that might mean.

"I need to get a proper look at you," Jonathan said. He slipped the blade under Tony's shirt and parted it in a single motion. His brother's chest was a mass of bruises; yellow and red, black and purple and blue.

"Who did this to you?" Jonathan asked. He didn't listen for an answer, there never was one. Not one he believed anyway. He started to examine him.

Tony hissed and bucked beneath his touch. "Sorry," Jonathan said quietly, but carried on with his assessment. Two cracked ribs at least, probably more. The bruises looked to be a couple of days old so, although they probably hurt, they couldn't be the source of the blood.

"What did you do?" Jonathan asked.

"Fell down the stairs." Tony laughed, but the response caused him to wince with pain.

"Jesus, Tony. What would Mum say?"

"She'd say, 'You've got yourself mixed up in a right mess once again, Antony. It's a good job you've got a brother to rely on.'" Tony laughed. Over the years they'd both become excellent mimics and for a moment their mother could have been standing in the corner of the room, watching them.

"What is it?"

"Shit, that hurts," Tony said through clenched teeth.

"What does? Where are you bleeding?" Jonathan started probing with his fingers again. At the edge of his vision he was conscious of the sticky red pool of blood. That didn't come from any cracked ribs. He moved his examination to his brother's head and neck, gently feeling with his fingertips for a wound.

"Help me, Tony. What happened?"

"Have you got any ..." Another bout of coughing halted Tony mid-sentence. "Any morphine in there?"

Jonathan shook his head. A flashing thought crossed his mind that this was a put-up job.

No, Tony was clean. Tony had been clean for months now. But the nagging doubt remained – the recognition that when Tony was deep in the hole, and there were times when Tony had been *deep* in the hole, nothing was impossible.

"Sorry Bro, just standard issue paracetemol and aspirin."

"Let me have those then."

"Where does it hurt?"

"Everywhere." Tony bucked his body against the pain again – another three thousand volts through his nerves – and this time he screamed.

Jonathan had never heard his brother scream before. Despite everything they'd been through – broken legs and a punctured lung and heroin withdrawal – he had never heard his brother scream.

He took Tony's wrist and checked his pulse. Tony's skin was hot, not just warm but hot, and when he found his pulse he knew it had to be a mistake because it was racing too fast for him to be able to keep up with it. *Onetwothreefourfive. Jesus, was that one fifty a minute? Faster?*

He felt something twitch beneath his fingertips and the shock snatched his hand away from Tony's wrist. *What was that?*

He reached for his phone.

"What are you doing?"

"Getting you an ambulance."

Tony knocked the mobile from his hand. It skittered across the floor and clattered against the skirting board.

"It's too late for that."

"Don't be stupid. I can't help you this time, Tone. I can't even take your fucking pulse." He reached out again and put his fingers over the pressure point. The pulse thrummed against his skin and he tried not to imagine the pressure Tony's heart must be under.

Once again Jonathan felt the skin shift under his touch, but this time he didn't remove his hand. He wasn't expecting it, but the sensation didn't take him so much by surprise. The motion felt strange and he tried quickly to analyse it. Hard, like a stone; and rounded, as if a pebble had passed under his fingers. But that didn't make any sense.

"What is it?" Jonathan asked.

At first he thought Tony wasn't going to reply – either because he hadn't heard him or because he was too far gone.

"Wrangling," Tony eventually said. Softly, like a breath of air, so that Jonathan wasn't even sure he'd heard his brother correctly. "They told me it was safe." He laughed, and the motion jolted his whole body. The pool of blood was large and bright red against the pale lino floor and Jonathan thought the movement had added a few more millilitres of liquid to the spill. Tony was still bleeding from somewhere.

"Safe," Tony whispered. "Yeah, and I'm the fucking Pope. But I needed the money."

"I could have given you the money."

Tony shook his head. "Not like this. No more chump change, Johnnie, I was big league."

Jonathan shuddered at the thought of what Tony meant by big league. Guns instead of knives. Crack instead of Marijuana.

"Big league, sure," Jonathan echoed back. It wasn't his imagination – Tony's voice was getting quieter. He had to lean in close to hear him properly.

"Don't leave me." Tony whispered. "I don't want to die alone."

"You're not going to die." But as soon as he said the sentence aloud he recognised the lie. Even with the bruises and the blood smeared across his face he could see that Tony was noticeably paler.

"Is it bad news, Doc?" Tony asked. His tone suggested he already knew the answer.

"Who did this?" Jonathan asked.

"Bastids."

"What?"

Tony tried to struggle into a sitting position. At first Jonathan tried to stop him – lying down was at least reducing the rate at which the blood fled from his body – but he quickly realised that he could either help Tony or fight him. He put his hands into Tony's armpits and pulled him upright.

Tony looked down at his chest.

"There."

The skin on Tony's chest rose in a small bump. Jonathan watched the shape travel down the breastbone and then disappear. It made Jonathan think of a submarine diving below the surface of the ocean. He watched the expanse of Tony's chest and a moment later another pebble appeared near his shoulder and began to travel down his left arm.

"Bastids," Tony said. "They've got a proper name – a long scientific name. You'd like it. But I just call them Bastids."

"What are they? Parasites?"

"You could say that. Fucking parasiting me anyway." He paused for a moment and Jonathan realised Tony's breath smelled of raw meat and old blood.

"Don't say any more," Jonathan said.

"No." The word came out strangled with wet air. "You need to understand."

"I understand enough."

"No you don't. They paid me to look after them, feed and care for them. One thousand pound a head for every live one."

"What for?"

"Fighting."

Jonathan had an image of two boxers in a ring, squaring up to one another whilst the pebbles of hard flesh shifted beneath their skin.

"Like dog fighting," Tony said. "Only with Bastids." He grinned. There were tiny flecks of blood on his front teeth.

The image in Jonathan's head changed – from Marquis of Queensbury rules and a sports stadium to some grubby dirt floor in a barn in the middle of nowhere; a handful of naked bulbs shining down on the ring and the stink of blood and faeces and rank sweat thick in the air. He ached at the recognition that this second image fitted so much better with Tony.

A pebble – *Bastid*, Jonathan's mind quickly replaced – rolled down Tony's left cheek and for a moment it bulged in his throat, the skin around its hard body pulled taut.

"These are just babies – and a bastard to care for." Tony laughed at his own joke. "You ought to see the daddies – all claws and armour. Vicious as fuck." There was something in his voice – it took Jonathan a moment to recognise it. Pride.

"What did you do?"

"Accident," Tony said. "Got too cocky, din't I? Mum always said that would be my undoing." He paused and Jonathan thought he was trying to find the energy to carry on talking.

"Hush." Jonathan reached out and took his brother's hand into his own. It was strange – he'd expected a soft, childlike hand and instead he felt the rough palm of a man. It occurred to him that they had probably not held hands since they were kids – crossing the street on the way to school or jumping off the high board in the swimming baths.

"I don't want to die," Tony said. His voice was small and childlike and he was no longer the hard man that slightly scared Jonathan. All that was swept away and they were kids again. Just brothers.

"It could be worse," Jonathan said. He was trying not to cry, but he could feel the strain in his words as he spoke.

"How?"

"You could have died a Derby fan."

Tony laughed. The sound was so slight and pitiful it was terrible. "Don't let me go," he whispered.

"Never."

Tony squeezed his hand.

Jonathan looked into his brother's eyes. The sclera was bright red – filled with fresh blood. *Not long now.*

He had witnessed so many deaths in his time that it was impossible for him to number them: old men and women wasting away in care homes, deaths from cancer and heart attacks. He had seen people who had accepted death as a final release and others who had fought against biology to the very end. He had seen a small girl waste away to nothing. He had seen both of his parents die. But Tony was his brother. His younger brother. He wasn't supposed to die first. He wasn't supposed to die at all.

"I'm sorry, Bro," Jonathan said. "I let you down."

Tony closed his eyes and Jonathan was sure his words had gone unheard, but then there was a tiny twitch at the side of Tony's mouth. "You always did," he said with a smile.

And died.

Jonathan recognised the moment. There was something so definite, so certain about death that it was almost impossible to mistake. Tony's body relaxed ever so slightly as he sank back to the floor. Jonathan kept hold of Tony's hand but even as he did he could feel the warmth fleeing from his brother's skin.

He used his left hand to wipe away the moisture around his eyes. The movement was awkward but he couldn't use his right hand – it was still holding tightly to Tony.

"I let you down," he said again, and this time Tony wasn't there to argue with him or make a joke of it. The words fell flat and hard in the kitchen.

Jonathan might have remained sitting beside his brother's body all day, all week, if it hadn't been for the noise. A soft mewling, like a hungry kitten – first one voice and then many. He looked up, shifting his head to try and get a sense of where the sound was coming from. And all the while he held tight to Tony's hand.

The noise grew louder. Did Tony keep a pet? A cat or maybe a dog that somehow understood that its owner had passed? Jonathan was embarrassed to realise he wasn't sure. How could he not know if his brother kept any pets?

In the end he stood up, reluctantly folding Tony's hand across his chest. He stared at his brother's skin a while longer, but if there were any more of the Bastids around they were buried deep within his body. A rage of anger passed over him – *I'm going to find who did this to him and make them pay*, but he almost laughed aloud at the absurdity of the vow – it was the plot for a bad Van Damme movie. He was a GP and the men who Tony had been working with ... well, they were *bad*. They'd take one look at the avenging doctor and then rip him to bits.

Shame rolled over him in hot, bright waves. Shame and frustrated impotence. *Go back to your surgery and your flu jabs and your diabetes tests, this isn't for you.*

"No," Jonathan said. He spoke softly, quietly, as if he was afraid that they might be listening in the next room. "No. I won't let it go."

The animal noises grew louder. They reminded him of the screech that mating foxes made. If he didn't shut them up soon the neighbours would call the police. Jonathan looked around the kitchen – at the slab of his dead brother lying on the ground surrounded by a pool of blood. How to explain what had happened here to the police?

He left the kitchen and returned to the hall. He tracked the sound along the corridor and stopped at a door fitted into the side of the stairs. There were five padlocks holding the door shut. And two deadbolts.

"What were you keeping in here?" Jonathan asked his dead brother. A small nail jutted out at a skewed angle from the woodwork beside the door – as if it had been driven into the wood in a hurry. Just like Tony, always too much haste. Hanging from the nail was a bunch of keys.

The first key Jonathan tried fitted the third padlock. He went through the keys until he had the five padlocks lying open on the ground beside his feet.

He reached for the first of the two deadbolts and pulled it out of its housing. He heard a rapid chittering, as if whatever was on the other side of the door was excited by his arrival.

And then it hit Jonathan: The padlocks weren't to keep anyone *out* of the cellar – if that was the case then why leave the keys beside the door? – the locks were to keep whatever was behind the door safely inside.

He rushed back to the kitchen. Lying on the floor next to Tony's body were the heavy gloves and the welder's mask. He dropped the mask over his face and was immediately hit with the odour of Tony's body. He pulled on the gloves – the insides were moist, coated with his brother's sweat. It was like pulling on Tony's skin. The observation was not as uncomfortable as he would have expected.

Jonathan looked around the room. Boots. Tony was wearing thick rubber boots. He bent down and pulled them off his brother's feet, revealing bright red socks.

He pulled on the boots and clomped out of the kitchen to return to the door beneath the stairs. The helmet echoed his own breathing back at him, but beneath this he could still hear the chittering and mewling.

He took a deep breath, drawing in a lungful of eau d'Tony, and snatched at the bolt. The door held tight to its frame, as if the wood had warped, and he had to pull hard before it opened.

The stench of rotting meat rolled out through the open door and he recoiled. The smell, warm and wet, stung his eyes and coated the back of his throat.

"Jesus, Tony. What the hell have you been messing with?"

Darkness spilled over the top step of the cellar and seeped into the hallway. Jonathan looked through the doorway. He could see the first five steps leading down into a pool of black air.

Jonathan pulled off a glove and reached out. At full stretch his fingertips touched the frame of the doorway and then he leaned inside and felt about for a light switch. The hard plastic felt alien beneath his skin but he felt a surge of relief – for a moment there he thought he'd have to go down and investigate the cellar in the dark. The idea was too appalling to consider.

He pressed down on the switch. The loud plastic click brought nothing. No light. He tried again – clicking it back and forth.

"Hell."

He moved closer to the top step and looked down into the cellar. Darkness swirled below him like a bottomless pool.

I'm not going down there. I can't go down there. Leave it for the police to sort out.

"*Coward.*" Tony's voice – loud and clear, as if his brother was standing beside him. Standing beside him and taunting him to take his turn on the rope swing, or daring him to run across the main road, or challenging him to swipe a handful of penny chews from the corner shop when Mrs Linday's back was turned.

Coward.

"I let you down," Jonathan said, but he wasn't sure which disappointment he was referring to – standing at the side of the road with his knees locked in fear, coming out of Linday's shop with empty pockets, or walking into the bright yellow kitchen to find his brother dying in a pool of his own blood.

He walked slowly back to the kitchen and stood over Tony's body. "I let you down. Mum told me to look after you, and I let you down."

Tony said nothing. No taunts this time. Jeers had never been able to change his mind anyway – they'd hurt, like tiny steel barbs in his skin – but he'd still stood by the side of the road or handed the rope to the next boy in the line.

"Sorry," Jonathan said. He walked over to the other side of the room, bent down to pick up his mobile phone, and walked back to the cellar.

The smell had escaped the cellar and infected the rest of the house. It conjured images in Jonathan's mind – of fly-blown meat with blue and yellow streaks through it, and congealed fat at the side of a plate. He tried to breathe through his mouth but stopped almost immediately – he could taste the foetid air at the back of his throat.

He turned on his phone. The wan light slipped over the stone steps.

He heard another noise – scratching, like nails on brick. He hesitated on the top step, and then had to turn round to check there wasn't a line of nine year old boys waiting behind him and Tony at the back, urging him on.

He took three steps down into the cellar, and then paused to hold the phone out in front of him. His muscles were tight; his arm locked into place. He realised he was half expecting a hand to emerge from the darkness and take the phone from him.

There was still nothing to see. Just the pool of seething blackness. No end to the steps that led down. Except ...

Jonathan peered into the dark. He thought he saw something. Movement. He panned his phone in front of him, spreading out the light like a weak searchlamp. Nothing definite. Nothing conclusive. But... something.

He took another step. And another.

The air trapped inside the mask was hot and moist. Beads of sweat formed on the inside of the visor and he felt others trickling down the side of his face. He wanted to lift the mask for a second to cool down, just for a second, but he resisted.

He took another step. *Just how deep was this cellar?* For a moment he felt certain that this was not another of Tony's dodgy business decisions. He hadn't cut a deal with some run-of-the-mill thug this time. No, Tony had outdone himself in his latest endeavour and made a deal with the devil himself.

Jonathan laughed at the idea, but the sound came back to him, marbled and redoubled in the confines of the cellar, and it sounded like mockery. Jonathan fell silent.

The light from the phone flickered and for a second he was left in absolute darkness. The stench rushed in. The scratching sound of nails upon stone grew louder.

"No," he whimpered. He shook the handset. The light returned, stronger than before.

On the step below Jonathan there was a car battery with two wires leading from the terminals. He traced them along the crumbling wall, to a makeshift switch.

Jonathan reached out and turned on the rig, and the cellar exploded with illumination.

Huge lights were strung across the roof, connected by spaghetti wiring – another of Tony's DIY jobs. Sharp white light pressed down and Jonathan raised his hand to shield his eyes from the glare.

At first there was only the light – burning through every detail. Slowly, Jonathan's eyes adjusted.

The floor was just a few feet below him. And seething with black pebbles: Bastids. *They were inside Tony?* he thought.

The animals crawled over each other, three and four layers deep. At the edges they were even thicker; trying to find purchase to climb the walls.

There was a lump of them almost at the base of the stone staircase. Jonathan looked around and noticed more mounds spread around the floor of the cellar. As he watched, a wave of Bastids fell from one of the structures and revealed the shape beneath them.

The remains of a dog. White ribs picked clean of flesh. The tiny creatures wound through the carcass. The head had been partially stripped, just enough to disguise what breed it had been. Jonathan assumed something large – an Alsatian or a Sheepdog.

"What the hell did you get yourself caught up in?" he whispered.

Further away, another carcass – this one more recent, with some skin and muscle still hanging onto the bones. Jonathan thought about his brother lying dead in the kitchen upstairs. He imagined him dressed up in his thick gloves and rubber waders, trudging across the floor with a dead dog on his back and then dropping it on the floor for the Bastids.

"Oh, Tony."

He looked down and one of the creatures had managed to climb the bottom step and was slipping across the toe of his boots. Jonathan shrieked and kicked out. The creature flew back into the mass but the movement caused Jonathan to overbalance and for an instant he was sure he was going to fall headfirst into the seething throng of black bodies.

And what then? Whatever had happened to Tony.

All this for what? So short, fat men could stand around a circle in some off-the-map farm and watch these creatures fight each other? What sort of sick bastards were they? Tony was an idiot for getting involved with them, but Tony had been desperate. They *were the evil ones. They were the ones who made this happen.*

At the foot of the stairs was a white coal sack, the mouth folded closed. Jonathan opened the sack and looked inside. Black and purple chrysalides, each as long as his forearm. So these were the adults? Hibernating now. Growing. Two of the cocoons had split open.

It occurred to Jonathan that at some point Tony's *friends* would come here, to collect their merchandise. If he did nothing then they would find Tony's body in the kitchen and half a million of their investment writhing in the cellar. And what would they think about Tony's death? Nothing. Or worse than nothing – one less expense to have to worry about.

"It's not going to happen."

Jonathan stumbled back up the steps and out into the hallway. He snatched the mask away from his face and the air smelled sweet and fresh.

He walked into the kitchen. From the corner of his eye he saw a flash of movement. Just a mouse. A rat. The house was probably riddled with them.

Tony's body lay sprawled across the floor. The skin on his chest flexed as one of those *things* burrowed underneath. Even as Jonathan watched the skin cracked and he saw the silvery-black carapace of one of the creatures begin to emerge from the body.

And Jonathan knew. Didn't just guess but *knew*. He could see the men who would come here to find Tony's body – not the soft money men with their pasty skin and paunches, but the thin and desperate workers, hard men like Tony had been. It wouldn't take them long to make the decision and then they would drag Tony's body across the floor and down the steps into the cellar. Because although there had never been much meat on Tony, food was food.

"No." He shook his head wildly. As if the men were in the room there with him. "Never."

He stomped on the creature as it fell off Tony's body. For a moment the black carapace resisted his weight. He could feel it writhing under his boot. And then the shell broke with a loud snap. Green-grey fluid seeped out from the broken body and across the floor.

Jonathan stared at his brother's body and although he was certain there were more of the creatures in there, his skin was still.

Jonathan unlocked the back door and walked out to the garage. What he needed was hidden under the tarpaulin at the back. The drum of turps was half empty, but when Jonathan unscrewed the cap the sting of the fluid was sharp.

He dragged the plastic drum through the kitchen and into the hallway. He wasn't a smoker, and Tony had not been either. For all his vices, that was one habit his little brother had failed to latch onto. In the end he found a box of Swan Vestas on a shelf above the cooker. He opened the cardboard box and discovered more burnt heads than live matches, but he figured that he only needed one to light.

He started to drag his finds down the cellar steps. One of the creatures had managed to drag its little body as high as the third step – God alone knew how – and Jonathan took great pleasure in crushing the little fucker beneath the rubber soles of his boots and then kicking the body back down the stairs.

He twisted open the turps drum and then stood there for a moment like the world's greatest idiot, looking for a place to set the cap down. He laughed – a sound that didn't strike him as entirely sane – and then threw the cap into the thrum of shuffling black bodies. He began to tilt the drum, hanging over the bottom step to try and cast the liquid as far across the cellar floor as possible.

"No! Johnnie, No!"

The voice came down the cellar steps, as loud as if Tony had picked up his body and dragged it across the kitchen floor to the door at the top of the cellar. Jonathan even turned and looked up, expecting to see his little brother lying there looking down at him.

The top of the stairs was empty, but for just a minute there ... for just a minute Johnnie had believed his brother had come back.

"I'm doing it for you," Johnnie said.

"Not like this."

A detached part of Jonathan's mind wondered how much of this was real. Whether he could actually hear his dead brother speaking to him, or if it was simply a voice conjured up by his own mind. But most of him didn't care. Most of him heard Tony and realised he had at least another couple of seconds with him.

"What should I do?" Johnnie asked.

"Don't burn them," Tony said. Johnnie heard something in his brother's voice he didn't recognise. Was it ... love? He looked at the animals scrabbling around on the floor beneath him. It was inconceivable that anyone could ever love them. They weren't fluffy rabbits or cute dogs; they were hard and vicious and lethal.

"They did this to you," Johnnie said.

"It isn't their fault."

"Then whose fault is it?" Jonathan asked.

The silence at the top of the stairs was terrible.

"Not mine?" Johnnie asked.

No response. Jonathan thought about his brother's cold body lying on the yellow lino in the kitchen.

"I told Mum I'd look after you."

And you did. He was desperate to hear Tony reply, to tell him that he was exonerated. That it didn't matter that he'd gone off to university and left him behind. That it wasn't his fault he wasn't able to protect his little brother.

"I tried," Johnnie said. "I did everything I could."

"Did you?"

"You know I did."

"All I know is that you left me."

"What do you want me to do?" Johnnie asked.

Feed Them.

Johnnie reached his hand into the white coal sack. He pulled out the two empty chrysalides and dropped the empty husks onto the ground. *They* were no use to him. The next one he picked up was heavy and shifted in his hand. It reminded him of Mexican Jumping Beans. *Did they really have a live worm inside them?* He'd never known whether to believe what Tony told him.

He fetched a knife from the kitchen and inserted the blunt tip under the tough skin and started to prise it open. The skin peeled back easily, as if it were ripe; ready to open.

There were three of them, lying side by side in a line and they reminded Johnnie of peas in a pod. Three small black creatures. Fragile things, not much longer than the kitchen knife.

"Is this it?" Johnnie asked. "Is this all it is?" He couldn't see what all the fuss was about, they looked less frightening than their pebble-like babies. He thought of what Tony had told him – about how men gathered around them like kids in the school playground chanting fight-fight-fight. He couldn't imagine anyone wanting to see these small things attack each other.

He tipped the first two directly into the opened ice-cream tub. The motion stirred them but they were drowsy and easily handled. Now that they were out of their cocoons he could see them more clearly. They had tiny claws at the front of their bodies, a hard black carapace. At the rear was a tail, almost as long as the body and with a wicked spike at the end. It began to twitch as they roused and Johnnie slammed the lid closed on them. The tail looked like it might hurt.

There was still another creature in the chrysalid. A yellow eye opened. Johnnie reached out to grab the animal whilst it was still sluggish. His hand tightened around the body of the animal.

And he screamed.

The pain was unlike anything he had ever felt before, as if someone had buried a poker into the soft flesh of his palm. He could feel the bastid burrowing into his hand, could feel those pincers chewing up skin and muscle and then bone. He opened his fist but the creature hung suspended from his palm. Johnnie tried to shake it free but it held tight to him.

Johnnie heard the hard clack of its pincers. He could feel the animal gripping onto him and the bright, hot flush of blood covering his palm. It was eating him. Eating into him.

Johnnie was crying. He could hear his own voice from a long way away, as if it belonged to someone else. He was aware that if he did nothing then the animal might simply burrow right through him. The image of the skeletons of the dogs rose to his mind. Is that what would happen to him?

He grabbed at the body of the bastid. His fingers slipped on the smooth chitin, lubricated with his own blood, and he couldn't find anything to grip. Each time he touched the animal it burrowed deeper until he was sure he could feel the pincers scratching against the bones of his hand.

Not that he could feel anything properly any more. His hand was a pool of molten pain, as if it had been dipped into a bucket of fire.

He grabbed again at it. And failed. Now when he looked down at his hand he could see flashes of white bone amidst the blood and muscle. The back of the animal sat neatly in his palm, as if it had fashioned itself a nest from his hand. His fingers clawed at the back of the bastid and slipped off.

Johnnie picked up the knife.

He started to hack at his own hand. His aim was not always accurate – sometimes the tip of the knife struck the back of the creature and sometimes it plunged directly into his own muscle, but he carried on stabbing. Stabbing down into the meat of his own hand.

Johnnie sat on the bottom step of the staircase. He held the white ice-cream box close to his stomach, cradling the container as if it contained a life's supply of football cards or marbles. Occasionally the container twisted in his grip and, once, the lid worked loose and a small, black claw reached out. He slammed his good hand down on the lid fast.

Sometimes he sang as he sat there. It helped to pass the time.

The bullies would come. The bullies who had hurt his little brother. And he would stand up to them. He would give them what they came for.

The box shivered on Johnnie's lap.

Feed them, Tony has asked of him. And he would.

Hersham Horror Books

Always The Baby

Sara Jayne Townsend

The end came much quicker than anyone expected. Three months after Mum was first diagnosed with cancer, she was gone.

For weeks I walked through life in a state of shock, but I knew I had to pull myself together for Abbie's sake. She went to pieces, the same way she did when Dad had died ten years earlier. But then, we'd had Mum to hold us up. Now Mum was gone and it was down to me to be the strong one. To be the big sister.

Mum hadn't had a will when she got sick, and had refused to discuss the matter whenever it was mentioned. I think she had to hold onto the belief that she was going to get well. Eventually her solicitor drew up a basic will leaving everything to me and Abbie, and persuaded her to sign it.

So Abbie and I had the house. When I did eventually get her to discuss it, I suggested that the best thing to do would be to sell it and split the cash evenly. "But we have to clear it out first," I said.

"It'll take ages," she argued. "And going around the house, knowing that Mum's not in it any more … it'll be unbearable."

"I know. But we need to sort things out before we get the house clearers in. There's probably stuff we both want. Mementos. Things we don't want being thrown away."

We agreed to start the following Saturday. I picked Abbie up in my reliable little Volkswagen. As usual, her car was being fixed. Abbie was hopeless with anything mechanical. She owned a powder blue Renault Clio, but it was always breaking down.

She was wearing designer jeans and a pink LaCoste T-shirt. "I said wear old clothes," I said. "We're going to get very dusty."

Abbie fixed me with a stare. "These are old."

To Abbie, of course, anything more than six months old counted as 'old'. She always looked effortlessly stylish, even when she was just allegedly throwing old things on. I'd given up trying to compete years ago. I was wearing a misshapen T-shirt covered in paint, and jeans that had holes in both bum cheeks and a big rip in one knee.

It was the first time we'd been back to Mum's house since she went into hospital. Even from the outside, I thought it looked sad. Abandoned and forgotten. I unlocked the front door and as I stepped over the threshold, arms laden with the boxes I'd brought to pack stuff up into, an overwhelming sense of emptiness consumed me. This was the house I'd grown up in, but for the first time in my life it didn't feel like home. It was just a collection of bricks and mortar. The soul had gone from it.

And it was quiet. For a long time I couldn't work out why the silence seemed so wrong. And then I realised. The clock on the living room wall wasn't ticking. It was battery operated. The battery had died, and no one had been around to change it.

I could already see the tears welling up in Abbie's eyes as she stared hollowly around the living room, everything neatly in place as it was when Mum was still living there. Her knitting in a bag beside her favourite chair. The family photos on the wall.

I steered Abbie into the kitchen. I could feel a trembling behind my own eyelids, but if I couldn't hold it together myself, there was no way I could expect Abbie to.

A calendar showing picturesque English scenes was displayed on the wall, in the place where I remembered a similar calendar hanging every year of my life. A sob escaped Abbie's throat. The calendar was still displaying August, the month Mum had gone into hospital. We were now into October, but there had been no one to turn the pages. It was a reminder of the lifeless husk this house had become, a house that had once been a home, so cosy and safe and welcoming.

I dumped the boxes onto the kitchen table and pulled the calendar off the wall. "You start in here. Put the crockery in the boxes. We can take it to the charity shop."

"All of it?"

I extracted one black sack from the roll I'd brought with us and shook it out. "Let's start a box each, for stuff that we might like."

"What if there's something we both want?"

"I'm sure we can come to an arrangement without turning into vultures. Anything that's trash, we'll throw away." I emphasised the point by stuffing the calendar into the trash bag. "Everything else, we'll leave for the house removal company to clear away."

Abbie opened a cupboard full of cups and glasses. "Where will you be?"

"I thought I'd start upstairs. Sorting out Mum's clothes." I extracted another two black sacks.

As I headed upstairs the house felt cavernous and unfriendly, and for the first time I found myself wondering why Mum had chosen to remain in a four-bedroom house by herself once everyone had gone. The rooms that had belonged to me and Abbie were shells – still with the beds and the furniture we'd used, but stripped of all the personal items they looked abandoned and forlorn. The door of the smallest bedroom was closed, the way it had remained for years. Too many bad memories. It had been Bethany's room, but Bethany drowned in the bath when she was a year old. Then there had been Sean, but he died of cot death at six months old. Mum and Dad never had any more children after that. Dad had redecorated the room and turned it into a study, but nobody could bear to spend any time in it after that.

I went into Mum's room and opened the wardrobe, staring at the contents. Mum had been a bit of a hoarder, and there was a lot of stuff crammed into it.

I couldn't bear to go through it. Everything I touched brought back a memory of Mum wearing it. The faded red jumper that was her favourite to wear around the house, warm and cosy watching TV while she did her knitting. The midnight blue evening gown with sequins that she wore to formal dinners with Dad – it hadn't fitted her for fifteen years but she looked so gorgeous in it she couldn't bear to throw it out. The checked red and white skirt that was a favourite for wearing out shopping in all seasons – teamed with a cheery red sweater in winter, and a sleeveless white top in summer.

In the end I just swept up armfuls of clothes and stuffed them into the black sacks, coat-hangers and all, without going through anything. The bags got full very quickly, and I ventured downstairs to bring up the rest of the roll. Abbie was piling mugs into one of the cardboard boxes, stacking them carefully so they wouldn't get damaged. She glanced up at me and then looked away, but not before I saw the tears rolling down her cheeks. Neither of us spoke. I grabbed the plastic sacks and headed back upstairs.

When I got to the end of the clothes in the wardrobe I realised what a huge job I'd taken on. The wardrobe was still packed full of stuff – shoes; scarves; hats; and cardboard boxes, all stacked up along the back of the wardrobe, looking quite precarious now there was nothing hanging on the rail in front of them. I already had eight full black sacks, and I hadn't even begun on the contents of the drawers yet.

And I had no idea what was in those boxes. Some of them looked pretty age-worn. Most of them were shoebox sized. I picked a couple at random from the top, pulling them out carefully so I wouldn't send the whole pile toppling over. I sat on the bed and removed the lid of the first box.

It was full of junk from childhood – mine and Abbie's. Baby teeth sealed in plastic bags. A ratty clay ashtray, crumbling now, that I remembered making in primary school. Programmes from school plays. School report cards and old exercise books.

I got a few more boxes down and discovered similar items. These boxes were a record of the lives of our mother's children. Everything we had done, everything we had brought home, was recorded in this stack of boxes. And it wasn't just me and Abbie, either. There was Bethany's first teddy bear. Bethany's birth announcement. Sean's hospital bracelet.

Hypnotised, I pulled out more and more boxes, spreading them out over the bed and the floor, rummaging through the contents of each one and then piling it on top of another as I reached in the back of the wardrobe for the next one. Drawings I made as a child – portraying Mum and Dad as huge triangular figures, with little heads at the top and little feet at the bottom corners of the triangle. Always with big smiles. I drew myself as smaller figure, usually lumped in protectively between the two parents. Abbie appeared as an afterthought, scribbled hastily in the corner of the picture. Usually portrayed as a squalling babe with mouth open and eyes just screwed-up slits. I guess I had jealousy issues when Abbie first came into my life. I had been three. It's hard for a child of that age to see a world that doesn't revolve around them, and the sudden switch of attention from me to the new baby must have been hard to deal with.

Towards the bottom of the wardrobe I found a box sealed with tape. None of the other ones had been. The tape had rotted, and fell apart when I pulled at it.

At first glance, it looked like all the other boxes. Stuffed with childhood mementos and drawings. I pulled out two drawings initially thinking they were more of my artwork, but then realised they must have been Abbie's – we had very different styles, even as young children. In the first drawing, Mum and Dad were drawn as large figures – Dad wearing a suit, as we usually saw him wearing when he came back from work, Mum in a red dress. There were three smaller figures in the picture. The one with the straight brown bob was me, as I wore my hair in that style for most of my childhood. Abbie would have been the figure with the bunches. She had always liked her hair long, and my mother had insisted she wear it up. Both of these figures were smiling, clustered together, their stick arms touching. Right at the bottom of the picture was a very small figure with a disproportionately big head and wild curly hair. Bethany. She had been born with a full head of curls. The figure in the picture representing my youngest sister had slashes of red crayon where her eyes should be, and a round red circle for a mouth. Angry red lines emanated from all round her head. I couldn't work out what they represented. Bethany crying? I remembered she had been a restless baby, always crying and never sleeping through the night. Or perhaps this picture represented Abbie's jealousy for a younger sibling that had suddenly appeared and taken all the attention away from her being the baby. I had already seen similar sentiments expressed in my own early drawings, but Abbie's seemed much, much angrier. Certainly I remembered how jealous she had been of Bethany. She was always trying to hurt Bethany – slapping her, pushing her, hitting her with toys – the moment Mum's back was turned. I thought again about how jealous I remembered being of Abbie, when she was born. Abbie had been six when Bethany was born. She'd been the baby for longer. Had that made it worse for her?

   Underneath the drawing was another one, also done in crayon, bearing the hallmarks of Abbie's artistic talents. This one showed a small figure lying flat. Wavy brown lines emanated from the figure's head, and wavy blue lines were drawn liberally across the figure. Above the figure was a larger one, sporting pigtails, appearing to be standing over the first. The stick arms were drawn straight down, as if reaching for the figure lying down.

Or holding the other figure down. A chill ran through me as I looked at the picture again. The blue lines ... could be water. The brown wavy lines looked like the way a person's hair floated in the water. A person with curly hair, perhaps. A baby with curly hair.

What did I remember of the day Bethany drowned? Abbie and I had been squabbling about what to watch on TV, after Mum had taken Bethany off to give her a bath. Abbie, getting her own way once again, commandeering the remote. Then the phone rang. Mum had called down for me to keep an eye on the baby for a minute. I'd argued and sulked. Why was it always me who had to be the responsible one? Mum had been distracted by the phone call by then. Abbie said she'd do it and bounded off upstairs.

I'd seized my opportunity and pounced on the remote. It must have only been a couple of minutes later when I'd heard Abbie calling me from upstairs. "Steffie! Steffie!" She'd always called me Steffie when she was young. But I was still mad with Abbie about getting her way over the TV, and I'd ignored her. She kept calling me. I went outside so I couldn't hear her anymore. We had a rather fine swing in the garden. I started swinging, getting a pretty good rhythm going, playing my usual game of seeing if I could swing high and hard enough to propel the swing all the way over the top of the frame (I never managed it). Then I heard Mum's scream, full of terror. I struggled to stop myself, ramming my trainered foot into the dirt beneath the swing, kicking up clods of earth in a desperate attempt to slow myself down, all the while hearing Mum's desperate wails from indoors. Finally I'd launched myself off the swing to the ground, nearly twisting my ankle in the process, and I'd gone running inside to find out what was going on.

Mum was sitting on the floor in the bathroom, clutching Bethany's little body to her breast. The first thing I noticed was that the water had soaked her blouse, leaving a big wet patch, but she seemed not to notice. She was sobbing into Bethany's hair. Bethany's skin had turned blue, and her arms flopped by her side. Then I got scared.

I didn't notice Abbie until I turned around again. I think perhaps I had a vague notion that in such situations, you had to phone 999, and maybe I was going to pick up the phone. Abbie was standing in the hallway, her eyes wide, but her face curiously without expression.

I was terrified. But Abbie had not been. And I had completely forgotten about that, in the chaos and grief that followed. In fact I'd completely forgotten it until now.

A noise from the corridor made me start. Footsteps on the stairs. Then I heard Abbie say, "Steph?"

I stepped out into the corridor, pulling the door to behind me. "Yes?"

"I was just wondering if we should call it a day."

"Have you finished with the crockery?"

Abbie hesitated. "I've done all I'm going to get done. I feel like I've been at it forever."

"We've still got a lot of work to do."

"I know, but it's not as if the house is going anywhere. We can come back tomorrow. I'm going to a party with Steve tonight. I need to get ready."

I glanced at my watch. "It's only just gone three. Even you don't need five hours to get ready for a date."

"I'm full of dust and grease and I need a long soak in the bath. Besides, I'm going nuts from staring at crockery. I'm going to go to bed dreaming about that damn crockery."

"Okay, fine. We'll knock off for the day."

"I was going to ask if you'd like to come out with us tonight. The party's to celebrate Steve's brother graduating from Uni. One of his house mates is really cute. And single."

I sighed. "Are you trying to set me up again?"

Abbie looked wounded. "I only do it if I think it's someone you'll get on with really well. Steve's brother lives in a house share. This house mate is the same age as you. He's tall, dark, works out a lot, has a science degree, and loves science fiction."

A tall, dark and handsome sci fi geek. Abbie knew my type, all right. I thought about another Saturday night in my lonely flat, eating take away food and watching crap TV. "Okay, I'll come. It's not as if I've got anything else to do tonight."

Abbie smiled. Her smile lit up a room, and reminded me what it was everyone loved about her. "It'll be a good distraction from all of this," she said.

"I'll meet you downstairs in five minutes."

Abbie nodded and trotted off down the stairs. I retreated back into the bedroom. I threw the lids back on the cardboard boxes and shoved them haphazardly back into the wardrobe. I hardly dared think about what I had discovered and the implications it might have.

After dropping Abbie off at her flat I went back to my own home and soaked for a long time in the bath. I felt grimy, and it wasn't just from the ancient dusty boxes in Mum's house.

Abbie had told me that Steve was driving and they'd pick me up at seven. I'd met Steve in passing a couple of times, and even from the brief conversations I'd had with him, it seemed he was not Abbie's usual type. Yes, he was good looking and clearly spent a long time in the gym, but he also seemed to have a brain – something that Abbie's boyfriends generally seemed to lack.

Once we arrived at the party, Abbie wasted no time in introducing me to the sci fi geek. "Alan, I'd like you to meet my lovely sister, Steph," she said, and turned on her million-dollar smile.

Alan shook my hand politely. "Nice to meet you, Steph. So what do you do?"

"I'm an admin assistant for the local council." I always felt slightly self-conscious telling people what I did for a living. It really wasn't very exciting, especially compared to Abbie, who could tell people she was a model. Most of the photo shoots she did were modelling clothes for catalogue companies, and occasionally head shots for make-up adverts in women's magazines, but it didn't pay very well and she had a bar job to keep her going between modelling assignments. But saying you're a model sounds far more glamorous than being an office worker. Even when it came to that, I'd always felt like I was living in Abbie's shadow.

She'd glided off and left me with Alan. Already she had attracted a cluster of people keen to bask in the light that seemed to emanate from Abbie's angelic smile. It had been that way all through school. There was something about Abbie that made people clamour to follow in her wake, in the hope of picking up just a bit of the golden glow that she seemed to radiate.

Alan and I chatted for a while. He was a nice enough chap, but I wasn't getting any vibe that he was attracted to me. It didn't take me long to work out why. He was clearly smitten with someone else. She was, I gathered, the sister of another house mate – a medical student, with a mane of blonde curls, a shy smile, and an aura that radiated sweetness. When she passed, she flashed Alan a self-conscious smile and I could see that this girl already owned his heart. They hadn't got up the nerve to get it together yet, and it would appear that how they felt about each other was not yet public knowledge, but was clear that they were destined to be together. And he had eyes for no one else.

Sadly, that was often the way it was when I went to social events with Abbie. Living under her shadow for so long had always made me feel awkward and self-conscious. Abbie was very enthusiastic about matchmaking for me, and under the spell of that golden aura, many boys had been persuaded to talk to me, instead of staying in her light. Unfortunately when the spell wore off, the boys invariably decided they didn't find me that interesting after all.

There had been one boyfriend of Abbie's – when she'd been 18 – who appeared to have been immune to her charms, and after meeting me he'd decided he liked me better. We went out for about three months. I'd felt guilty about it, of course, and had to put up with screaming rages from Abbie – who accused me of stealing him from her. In fact it got so bad that I'd decided to break up with him – I liked the guy, but I didn't have feelings so strong for him I was prepared to choose him over my sister. In the end the decision was taken out of my hands, as he suddenly stopped calling me and just dropped out of my life. He didn't turn up again in Abbie's either. Perhaps he decided being involved with our family was just more trouble than it was worth.

I was ruminating on this as I sat on the worn sofa in the students' house, once more alone. Alan had found a few other people to talk to. Abbie was in her adoring circle as always, and I didn't know anyone else. I was nursing a can of lukewarm lager and trying to decide if anyone would notice if I just sneaked away and called a taxi to take me home. Then someone said, "a bit of a drag, isn't it?"

I turned to see Steve sitting on the sofa beside me. "Isn't it your brother's graduation party?"

"Yeah, and I don't get along very well with my brother." He was sitting very close to me, and he seemed slightly drunk.

"Abbie didn't mention that," I said.

"Abbie doesn't notice anything that doesn't revolve around her."

"That's a rather unkind thing to say about your girlfriend."

Steve sighed. "I know she's your sister and all, but she's a pain in the arse."

"Why are you going out with her, then?"

"I'm trying to work out how to tell her I want to finish it."

I stared at him. "You want to break up with my sister?"

He looked uncomfortable. "She has this aura. You must know. You first meet her, and she draws you in. She turns that smile on you, and makes you think you're the only person in the world. But it's all a façade. When you get a glimpse of the person underneath, it's a different story. She's shallow and self-centred and selfish. I like women with more substance."

I looked at him. "You're rather more astute than most of Abbie's boyfriends."

He smiled at me, and I suddenly noticed he had a beautiful smile. "Not that I want to sound big-headed, but I'm getting the impression I might be a bit brighter than most of Abbie's boyfriends."

"I can't dispute that," I said. "But you're talking about breaking my sister's heart."

"She'll get over me. There are lots of guys out there who'd feel all their Christmases had come at once if Abbie were to shine that adoring light on them. However, the situation is a bit more complicated." He was staring at me intently.

"In what way?" I was starting to fear the answer.

"Because I'm planning on dumping Abbie for her sister, and that will make things very awkward."

"Me?" I stared at him. "You like me? There's nothing special about me."

"You're a woman of substance, Steph. Deep and mysterious and I can tell there's all kinds of things bubbling under the surface."

"How can you say that? You don't know anything about me."

"I like what I've seen so far." He put his hand over mine, and I felt my heart start to race. "You intrigue me, Steph. I'd like to get to know you better."

"I think you're drunk."

"I might be, but not too drunk to be bullshitting. I know we've only just met, but I'm attracted to you. Your sister is attractive on the surface, but there's nothing underneath. You, I think, have many attractive layers. I'd like to get to know you."

I could feel her eyes on me, the hostility behind the gaze cutting through the air, almost a physical thing. I turned my head, unsurprised to see Abbie staring at me from the centre of her circle. I self-consciously pulled my hand out from under Steve's. "I'm flattered, but I think you've had too much to drink. And I think it's time for me to leave." I stood up.

He looked at me, crestfallen. "How are you getting home? I drove you here."

"I really don't think you should drive anywhere tonight. I'm going to call a taxi. You should stay here with Abbie. If you wake up in the morning and feel the same way, then maybe we can talk."

I could feel Abbie's eyes burning into my back as I left the room but I did not turn back to look.

I went home and straight to bed, but I couldn't sleep a wink. I lay awake for hours, my mind turning over Abbie's eyes burning into me at the party, and then back to what I'd found in Mum's house. The image of the child's drawing kept slamming into the front of my brain.

At about four am I gave up trying to sleep. I got up and dressed, put on my coat, collected my bag and car keys, and headed back to Mum's house.

The roads were quiet so early in the morning and I arrived at the house in no time at all.

I turned on the landing light and hurried up the stairs to Mum's bedroom, not even stopping to take off my coat. It was cold; I decided to keep it on.

The room was, of course, as I'd left it, the bed rumpled where I'd been sitting on it, the boxes shoved in the wardrobe. I pulled all the boxes out again, digging out those from the bottom of the pile that I hadn't got around to looking at yet. I took the lids off and tipped them up, scattering all the contents over the bed.

I wasn't even sure what I was looking for. Was I looking for evidence that Abbie had killed our baby sister, or evidence to reassure myself to the contrary? I wasn't sure. But that memory of the day Bethany died kept replaying itself over and over in my head.

And then, buried deep in the pile of junk I had dumped onto the bed, I found a diary. The kind that comes with a lock and tiny key, to reassure a little girl that her secrets are safe. Only, they're not because the lock always breaks and it doesn't take long to open even without a key.

I knew what it was before I opened it. Abbie had been keeping a diary since she was seven years old. But they were all in a box in her bedroom. Fingering this one, I was a bit confused. Why wasn't it with the others? Then I started to read it and I knew.

It was the year that Sean was born. Initially the entries were probably no different from any other child resenting a baby sibling. Except that Abbie was nine when Sean was born, and she should have been over the whole jealousy thing. Then two months before Sean died, this: *I hate the baby. Mummy's never got any time for me. I wish things could go back to the way they were before.*

There were then a couple of weeks of how much Abbie hated the baby – disturbingly so. Then an entry that read: *I went to talk to Mummy and she was in the baby's room. She was upset because the pillow was over the baby's head. She started crying and said that the baby would die if he slept with the pillow over his head. She shouted at Daddy because he put the baby to bed. Daddy shouted back. Then the baby woke up and started crying and they were both cross. I wonder how long the pillow has to be on the baby's head before he dies?*

A couple of weeks later, another reference: *Mummy and Daddy don't put the pillow with the baby anymore. But it's in the cupboard with the towels. If I stand on tippy-toe I can reach it.*

I dropped the diary. I couldn't breathe; it felt like there was a great lump in my chest. Why was Mum hiding all this away? She must have understood what it meant.

All around lay the contents of the boxes. I started sweeping them up and randomly throwing them back into boxes. I should never have come back snooping through all this stuff. What the hell had I been doing hunting for skeletons in the closet? Now they were out in the open, I wanted to put them back.

As I picked up another handful of old papers, a yellowed envelope poked out from them. It was sealed, and written in Mum's handwriting, on the front, was my name.

I stared at it. Clearly this was for me, but why had Mum not given it to me when she was alive?

The envelope was old and the seal had degraded. The flap came open easily. I extracted a sheet of lined note paper, and I recognised Mum's handwriting. There was no date on it.

Darling Stephanie

I know that it will be you who finds this, because after I'm gone it will be you left to sort through the house.

I also know that if you have found this, you will have found everything else, and because you are an intelligent girl you will understand the secret about your sister that I have been hiding from everyone for so long.

I suspected for a long time before I knew anything. The way she looked at Bethany with such hatred. I assumed that was normal sibling rivalry. Abbie was used to being the baby. We all thought it would pass.

The day I found Bethany in the bath, I was so full of grief it took me a long time to work out what had really happened. The fact the bathroom door was closed when I went back to it. The fact that Abbie's clothes were still wet when she went to bed that night. I blamed myself for leaving Bethany alone; I didn't put the pieces together. Until I was sorting out Abbie's room months later and I found the drawing, the drawing of her holding Bethany under the water.

I suppose I should have acted then. But having lost one child I couldn't bear to lose another. And I needed Abbie, as much as she needed me. I needed someone to look after. You were growing up then, starting to do your own thing. Abbie still wanted to be the baby, and I needed to mother her.

Then Sean came along – quite by surprise. I did worry. It's why I never left Sean alone with Abbie. I was afraid of what she might do. When he died of cot death, everyone accepted that explanation. When the grief had subsided, I suspected. But I never knew for sure. Until a few years later, when I had a notion to go looking through Abbie's old diaries. I suppose I already knew the truth, and by that point I needed her even more. She was always the baby. She needed to be the baby. I took the diary and all the other things that might make other people suspect and I hid them. I didn't want to lose her too. She's my baby.

Siblings

I only have one last request, Stephanie, and that is that you never reveal this secret. Take this letter, and the drawing, and the diary, and burn them.

Now that I am gone she only has you. You know her like I do, and you will understand how much she needs someone to look after her. Without you, she will be all alone. If you love me I ask you to please, please, take this secret to the grave.

With all my love,

Mum xxx

I dropped the letter to the floor and sat hunched on the edge of the bed, my head in my hands. I let the tears flow unhindered, followed by huge, racking sobs. It seemed like I sat there for hours, crying until I felt I was empty inside. I cried for my mother. I cried for my long-dead father, who never knew that one of his daughters killed two of her siblings. I cried for little Bethany and Sean, who never had a chance to live. And I cried for Abbie. Abbie who shone a light in my life I had basked in for years. Without Abbie's light, I would be forever in darkness.

When I had no more tears to cry, I felt too exhausted to drive home. I went to lie down on the bed in the spare room, the room that had been my bedroom, once upon a time, but there was nothing left of mine in it.

Somehow I managed to fall asleep.

I awoke with daylight filtering through the faded floral curtains. My eyes felt irritated, my throat raw from all the crying.

I went back into Mum's bedroom and began to gather up the things scattered across the bed. The pictures, the baby things, the diary. I picked up as many of the shoeboxes as I could, and carried them downstairs and into the back garden, where I piled them up in a bare patch of earth amongst the scrubby neglected grass. I went back and forth and back and forth, gathering all the boxes and adding them to the pile until they were all out in the yard. Then I broke up the old coffee table with the wobbly legs to create firewood, and set fire to the lot. I sat and watched my childhood burn, until nothing remained but a pile of blackened ashes. The evidence was destroyed. I had carried out Mum's final wish.

The task was exhausting and time consuming. By the time I arrived home, it was dusk. I ached everywhere, the smell of dust and ashes still clung to my clothes. I turned on the taps to fill the bath and stripped out of my clothes, stuffing everything in the laundry basket. I soaked for a long time, trying to scrub the burnt remnants of my childhood away. Trying to scrub away the past.

Now that the evidence was gone only I knew Abbie's terrible secret. It was a burden I had to carry to my own grave. It was Mum's last wish. She'd protected Abbie because she needed Abbie in her life. She needed Abbie to look after. And I would have to pick up this burden as well, because I needed Abbie too. The few friends I had were also Abbie's. I had no one in my life that hadn't first been attracted to Abbie's golden light.

That made me think about Steve. I'd not heard from him since Saturday night. No doubt he'd sobered up and reconsidered what he'd said to me. I'd not heard from Abbie, either. She was probably still annoyed with me.

But then on Tuesday evening she rang me. I had just arrived at the house again, resigned to do some more sorting out. I saw her name flash up on my mobile and my heart sank. But she was surprisingly cheerful. "Hey Steph, where are you?"

"At Mum's house. There's still a lot of work to do, you know."

"That's why I'm phoning. To find out if you were at the house tonight. I'm on my way over."

"Really?"

"Did you think I was calling for some other reason? Maybe you're expecting me to yell at you because I saw you and him on Saturday?"

"The thought did cross my mind," I said cautiously.

"I'm not wasting any more energy on Steve. He's gone."

"What do you mean, he's gone? Did he dump you? Or did you dump him?"

"It doesn't matter. He's gone. I've got my car back, so I'm on my way now. I'll be there in about half an hour. Shall I bring some takeaway? I haven't had dinner yet."

"Sounds good," I said, mollified. "I haven't either."

After I rang off the call I headed upstairs to carry on sorting out the stuff in Mum's bedroom. I reached the bedroom doorway and, suddenly, I knew. It wasn't just Bethany and Sean. Of course it wasn't. Once you start down that path, it's a slippery, slippery slope.

Mum must have known all along. And she'd passed it on to me. The letter had been destroyed, but its contents were burned onto my brain: *Now that I am gone she only has you. You know her like I do, and you will understand how much she needs someone to look after her. Without you, she will be all alone. If you love me I ask you to please, please, take this secret to the grave.*

With tears forming in my eyes, I sat down heavily on the end of the bed, feeling completely and utterly alone.

Hersham Horror Books

My Little Sister

Stuart Hughes

My name is Michael Brayford. I'm forty-two years old and I'm a scene of crime officer working with the Metropolitan Police Force.

This is my confession.

The call from my little sister came through while I was working the scene of crime. My mobile was on silent and she went through to voicemail. I picked it up later when removing my disposable gloves, shoe covers, and overalls. It didn't matter that I didn't get the message straight away because Lucy always rang me after the event, never before or during.

This scene of crime was a particularly messy one and I should know; I'd seen enough in my time. I'd been trained to assume the victim was still alive unless decapitated, decomposing, or incinerated. But what the training courses missed out was unless the victim was swimming in blood.

With experience I learnt exactly how much blood the victim needed to swim in ... and this victim, or rather these victims, had lost enough blood between them to fill a swimming pool.

A quick briefing on my arrival at the high-rise flat in Limehouse from DS Quigley, the Senior Investigating

Officer, allocated me the male victim. PC Bryson logged me in.

The flat was on the sixth floor of an unsavoury tower block and the lift was out of action. I made a mental note to start exercising more as I lugged my gear up six flights of stairs.

The man lay on the living room floor amongst a debris of books, newspapers, broken ornaments, and a congealing pool of blood. He had shoulder length brown hair, probably in his mid-twenties, and was clearly dead. Although the exact cause of death would need confirming at the post-mortem, there was little room for doubt. The victim was only wearing pyjama bottoms and his bare chest was covered in multiple stab wounds, as were his neck, shoulders and arms. Defence wounds were evident on the palms of his hands and fingers.

From what Quigley had said the other victim was female and just as dead. She lay in the kitchen, wearing only a nightie, also covered in multiple stab wounds. My colleague Gaynor was working the female victim.

"How you doing, Mike?" Quigley asked.

"About done," I said without looking up. I scanned the victim again whilst mentally running through my checklist – blood and body fluid samples, anything that might have DNA traces, fingerprints, anything missing that I'd expect to find at the scene. "Yeah, you can take the body."

"Need I ask?"

"It looks like what it is." I looked up. Quigley frowned, adding more lines to his weather-worn chiselled face. He'd been on the force a very long time but each murder seemed to touch him as much as the first. Quigley cared.

Quigley nodded, scribbled something in his notebook, and wandered off towards the kitchen.

I gathered my gear, being meticulous with all the samples and evidence I'd collected, and carefully made my way out of the flat. PC Bryson logged me out.

The view over the railings as I headed along the walkway to the stairs was depressing. Greying tower-block after tower-block. The view might have been better on a summer evening but it was getting dark as the October night drew in. I shivered and hurried down the stairs.

Relieved that my car remained where I'd left it, even more amazed that it remained undamaged, I handed my gear, evidence and samples to PC Martin, the Police Exhibits Officer, who put them inside the Forensic Investigation van. I removed my disposable gloves, shoe covers, and overalls and put them in the van too.

"Thanks," Martin said.

"Been a long day," I said.

Martin nodded. "Will Gaynor be long?"

"I shouldn't think so." I turned and walked towards my car. "See you tomorrow."

As I got into the car I took my mobile off silent and inserted it into its cradle.

That's when I noticed the two messages.

Driving away from the depressing scene of crime, I listened to the messages on hands free.

The first was from Stacey. She said she was missing me and wanted to know when she could see me again. Stacey wasn't my girlfriend, not really, and even though we'd spent two nights together, she wasn't my lover either. I guess you could say we were dating, but not seriously. At least I wasn't serious. We were up to six dates now and I hadn't made it to seven dates with any girl since my ex-wife walked out on me eight years ago. Stacey had left me a dozen similar messages in the last week and her tone showed her frustration. I couldn't blame her really.

The other message was from Lucy. My little sister. Simple and to the point. "Mickey, it's happened again. I'm so sorry. You're my big brother and I need you to fix it. Will you come fix it?" And that was it.

A lump caught in my throat at the sound of her voice and my eyes filled up.

Oh, Lucy, I thought. *Not again.* And then on the heels of that. *This has to stop, Lucy. It has to stop.*

Of course I went though. I think Lucy knew I would. There was never any doubt about that.

There were two of us growing up in Altrincham. Lucy and me.

But it's Lucy I want to tell you about.

Lucy was two years younger than me – two and five twelfths my junior if you want to be precise – but two years is good enough for me. She was a bubbly, energetic, fun loving kid, who would never shut up. I used to buy her gobstoppers to shut her up but it didn't work.

I guess you'd call her a tom boy. Lucy had a lot more strength than a little girl had any right to. And even though I was two years older, every time we play fought she got the better of me. She'd wear jeans and T-shirts at every opportunity and she'd scream blue murder whenever Mum tried to get her to wear a dress. "Mickey doesn't have to wear a dress," she'd say. "Why do I have to?"

"Because you're a girl," Mum would reply.

Siblings

"It's not fair," Lucy would say. My little sister would sulk for a while but she'd wear the dress; and she'd soon have it dirty and possibly torn as we found a way to escape from the wedding, or party, or whatever it happened to be, and play.

Mum died when I was nine and Lucy was seven. Lucy wore a dress to the funeral but I don't think Dad ever got her to wear another dress after that.

Lucy was the one to find Mum. It was a Wednesday and Dad was at work – he was working the afternoon shift at the castings foundry – and I had stayed after school for football practice.

The way Lucy told it then, and still tells it now, the mother of one of her friend's had given her a lift and she'd been dropped off outside our house. Lucy had skipped up the drive and gone to open the front door but had found it locked. That was odd, she thought (and I agreed with her) because Mum always left the door unlocked so that we could go straight inside when we got home from school.

But on this Wednesday, while I was at football practice, Lucy got home first and the door was locked.

So Lucy banged on the door, and called for Mum, but there was no response.

That's when Lucy dropped her satchel, got down on her hands and knees, lifted the letter box flap, and looked inside.

And that's when Lucy screamed.

She screamed and screamed and screamed ... and she was still screaming when our nice neighbour Mrs. Hitchcock came out to see what all the hollering was about.

Mum, it seemed, had tripped coming down the stairs and fallen all the way to the bottom, breaking her neck, both legs, and one arm in the fall.

Time heals all wounds, they say, but I'm not sure I agree with that. Time doesn't heal at all; you just find a way over time to get on with your life again. At least some people do.

I did; I threw myself into my football, trained hard, and got to play semi-professional for a few years.

Dad did, but not very well. Dad started drinking and the drinking would eventually kill him. And once again, when that happened, Lucy had to deal with it on her own because I was at Aston University by then.

But Lucy never did. I don't think Lucy ever found a way to get on with her life.

I have a lot of regrets. I regret not being able to make my marriage work. I regret the way I treat the girls I've dated since my divorce. They deserve better. Stacey deserves better.

But my biggest regret, by far my biggest regret, is that I stayed at school that Wednesday. If I hadn't gone to football practice, I would've got home before Lucy.

I would've been the one that found Mum at the bottom of the stairs, her arms and legs and neck twisted at impossible angles, her pink dressing gown rucked up around her waist.

I'd give anything for Lucy not to have found Mum that day.

But that's not how things panned out.

Lucy was the one to find our Mum.

Not me.

She was the one to find Mum dead at the bottom of the stairs … and that's when Lucy started to unravel.

On the way home from the Limehouse scene of crime, I got two calls. The first from Gaynor. We talked about the scene of crime for a while. Gaynor's initial findings on the female victim were the same as my findings on the male victim. There seemed little doubt they'd both been killed by the same perpetrator. Gaynor informed me the post-mortems were scheduled for tomorrow afternoon.

The second call came from Stacey. I went to answer it and then paused with my index finger less than an inch away from the green button. Stacey was a nice girl. Very attractive, great figure, funny and entertaining to be with. There had been no awkward silences on any of our dates and we seemed to have a lot in common. We'd had two great nights in bed and neither of us had got much sleep if you know what I mean. I really wanted to see her again ... but it wouldn't be fair. Work and Lucy had driven a wedge between my ex-wife and me and I didn't want the same thing happening with Stacey. I hit the red button.

Home was a modest two-up, two-down in Enfield. I pulled onto my drive at just after 10.00 pm and killed the engine. I listened to Lucy's message again and my eyes filled up.

"Mickey, it's happened again. I'm so sorry. You're my big brother and I need you to fix it. Will you come fix it?"

There was no way I wouldn't go and fix it for my little sister but this would be the fifth time now that I'd fixed it.

Oh, Lucy, I thought. *This has to stop, Lucy. It has to stop*.

I took my phone out of its cradle and ignored the flashing light informing me I had a message. I typed a text to Lucy – *On my way. See you in a couple of hours. Mickey x* – and pressed send.

To my little sister I was Mickey but Lucy was the only one who called me that. To everybody else I was Mike or Michael. Most people called me Mike. Stacey called me Michael and I kind of like that.

"Mike's short for Michael, right?"

"Yeah." I smiled as I remembered our first date at the *Old Wheatsheaf*.

"Then I'll call you Michael … that's if you don't mind."

"No," I said. "I don't mind."

It had been a long time since anybody had called me Michael and it felt good.

As I got out of the car I listened to Stacey's message.

"Hi Michael, I thought you were better than this. I really like you and I'd like to see you again but I don't want to waste time playing games. If you like me and want to see me again you know where I am. If you don't, have the courtesy to tell me it's over. Or text me. Just don't play me, Michael. I deserve more than that."

She was right. Of course, she was right. Stacey deserved better. She didn't deserve to be treated this way. Hell, she deserved better than me.

I pocketed my phone, unlocked the front door, and went inside. A quick shower, a change of clothes, and I'd hit the road.

Lucy needed me.

Hindsight is a wonderful thing, isn't it? Lucy may have started to unravel when Mum died but I didn't notice. The first signs were there with the kitten incident but, even then, I didn't recognise them for what they actually were. I didn't realise the significance of the kitten thing until the later incidents, and by then it was too late.

Dad bought the kitten about six months after Mum died. He was drinking by then but he hadn't collected his alcoholic membership card. He was close, I think, he'd got the application form, and he may even have had the pen in his hand, but he hadn't signed on the dotted line. Not then.

The kitten was meant for both of us, I think, but as soon as Lucy laid eyes on the small ball of black fur it was only ever going to be hers. Lucy's kitten.

I can still remember the day Dad brought the kitten home. I was out in the back garden kicking a football against the garage wall. Naturally right-footed, I'd been kicking the ball with my left for the last week and that practice was beginning to pay off.

So I was the first to see Dad as he pulled up the drive.

"Hey, Mike," he called.

I raised a hand in acknowledgement but kept my eyes on the football.

"Mike!" I looked up. Dad was carrying a small cardboard box. He deftly closed the car door with his backside and walked towards the house. "Come inside a minute."

I kicked the ball against the wall as hard as I could and followed Dad into the house.

"Lucy!" he called. "Here a minute!"

Dad went into the living room and put the cardboard box on the coffee table. Lucy sat on the sofa with her legs curled underneath her. The TV was on but she didn't seem to be paying it much attention.

"I've got something for you." Dad pointed at the box. It was one of those with four flaps that fold over and under each other securing the top.

Neither of us moved.

"Well?" Dad said.

I looked at Lucy. She was sitting on the edge of the sofa but made no move to get off. She tilted her head, her red hair floating through the air, and said, "Open it, Mickey."

So I did. I stepped forward and grabbed two of the flaps. The fit was tight and the box creaked and twisted on the table as I prised the flaps apart. From inside came a faint "Meow" and then, as I prised open the other flaps, an even louder "Meow!"

That got Lucy's attention. She jumped up and barged me out the way in her eagerness. For a moment she paused in front of the box and looked inside, bending forward at her waist to get a good view.

"Awww," she said. "It's so cute."

And it was. A black kitten with white paws and a white patch on its chest.

"Can I?" Lucy said, holding out her arms. She looked over at Dad. "Can I?"

"Go ahead," Dad said.

So Lucy scooped the kitten out of the box and held it against her chest. She had it under both front shoulders and its back legs dangled free. The kitten squealed and struggled.

"Put one arm underneath it," Dad said.

Lucy did and the kitten soon settled down. Before long it was purring as Lucy stroked its soft fur and beamed. I stepped forward, gingerly reached out a hand, and stroked the top of its head. When it didn't bite or scratch I got braver and stroked the soft fur on its back.

"What's it called?" Lucy asked.

"It's not an it, it's a she," Dad said. "And she doesn't have a name. Want to give her one?"

"Oh, yeah!" Lucy said, delighted. "What are we going to call her, Mickey?"

I shrugged. Lucy was holding the kitten tightly and it purred. We both stroked it.

"I've still got some stuff for the kitten in the car. Want to give me a hand, Mike?"

I helped Dad in with the cat litter tray, a couple of heavy bags of cat litter, plus two dozen tins of cat food. The food went in the cupboard. The litter tray went in the corner of the kitchen by the washing machine. The cat litter, when Dad poured it into the tray, looked like little stones.

"We'll store the cat litter bags in the garage," Dad said. He was still beaming and it had been a long time since I'd seen Dad smile.

By the time I returned to the living room, Lucy was on her hands and knees. She'd made a paper ball out of newspaper and was throwing it for the kitten to play with. Lucy looked up at me with big brown eyes and a huge smile.

"Boots," she said. "I'm going to call her Boots."

"Why?" I said. "That's a *stupid* name."

"No, it's *not*," she said, scooping the kitten into her arms. "She's got white boots. See?"

"Okay."

And with that Lucy named the kitten.

Boots became Lucy's kitten.

For a short while at least.

The novelty of the new kitten lasted about a week before Lucy started to lose interest. For that first week Boots and Lucy were inseparable and if Lucy could have taken the kitten with her to school she would've done.

Lucy doted on the kitten. She fed it. She gave it milk. She changed the cat litter tray, but most of all she fussed and played with it. I liked Boots too, and played with it whenever I could, but Boots always went to Lucy and only tolerated me when my little sister wasn't about.

Like I said though, that all changed after about a week. Lucy started to feed the kitten less and less and she completely forgot about the cat litter. So I started feeding Boots and it became my chore to empty and refill the litter tray.

At first Dad gave Lucy a hard time over it but he let it go after a few days when he saw that I was picking up the slack.

I could understand Lucy getting bored of the chores but she even lost interest in doing the fun things with the kitten. Boots still followed Lucy everywhere but my little sister ignored the kitten and then some. When Boots followed Lucy, my little sister would run to the door, quickly open it and hurry through, before closing the door so the kitten couldn't follow. And if Lucy was curled up on the sofa watching TV and Boots came to her for some fuss, Lucy would simply scoot the kitten off the sofa and onto the floor.

When I spoke to Lucy she said that Boots scratched her and bit her and that she didn't like the kitten any more. I'd seen no evidence of that at all. I was spending more time with Boots and she was as gentle and soft as anything. Yes her claws came out now and again when I played with her, especially when I tickled her tummy, but Boots had never scratched or bitten me.

The kitten never changed its allegiance though. Maybe if Boots had switched her affection to me or Dad then the kitten incident might not have happened. But she didn't. Boots never left Lucy alone and …

… well it happened one summer afternoon after school. The kitten incident. Dad wasn't home from his shift at the foundry. I was in the garden kicking a football against the garage wall. My left foot was nearly as good as my right by this time so I was alternating kicks, playing a game between my left and right feet. Lucy was in the garden too, behind the garage checking on the runner beans and other vegetables that were growing there.

I remember I'd just delivered a sweet kick with my left foot, that was too hot for my right to handle, and was running to collect the ball when I heard the squealing. A mewling sort of a squeal.

The ball had landed in the flower bed on the far side of the lawn. I stooped to pick it up and heard the squealing again.

"Lucy?" I called. And then a little louder, "Lucy!"

No answer.

I held the football in the crook of my left arm and walked towards the garage.

"Lucy!"

As I turned the corner and headed towards the vegetable patch I saw her. She was standing at the far side of the garage wall dressed in a white T-shirt and denim jeans, her arms out straight in front of her as if imitating Frankenstein's monster. Tightly gripped between both her hands was Boots. She had the kitten by the neck. I could see its black head and ears above Lucy's hands and the rest of its body, legs and tail dangled in mid-air.

At first I thought Lucy was playing with the kitten but Boots wasn't moving and Lucy wasn't smiling. Lucy's head was shaking from side to side in exaggerated movements, her red hair wafting in the cool breeze, but her arms remained ramrod straight.

"Lucy," I said and took a step closer. Followed by another step.

Lucy ignored me and continued to hold the kitten at arm's length.

I took another step and realised Lucy was talking to herself as she shook her head from side to side.

"Naughty kitten, naughty kitten, naughty kitten …"

I dropped the football and heard it thud a couple of times before coming to a stop.

"… naughty kitten, naughty kitten, naughty kitten …"

"Lucy!"

"… naughty kitten, naughty kitten …"

I stepped closer and saw the tear tracks down Lucy's cheeks.

"Lucy!"

"… naughty kitten, naughty kitten …"

I reached out and grabbed both of her hands in mine. I eased them apart and she didn't put up a fight, simply let me prise her fingers from the kitten.

"… naughty kitten, naughty kitten …"

Down on my knees I let go of Boots and released the kitten onto the ground. Boots didn't move. The kitten was stretched to its full length and its tongue poked out from the corner of its mouth. It didn't move. I watched its chest, looking for any sign of rise and fall, but couldn't see any. I reached out and rocked it slightly with my hand. There was no response.

Lucy was standing beside me now. She stretched out her right leg and kicked it.

"Lucy!"

"Is it dead?" she asked. Her voice hushed and choked with tears.

"I think so."

"Good. She was a naughty kitten. Look." Lucy stepped in front of me and held out her arms. Both her left and right inner forearms were covered in scratch marks. "See. She scratched me."

"But you killed her."

"I duh–" My little sister burst into tears. "I duh–" her voice hitched and the words wouldn't come. "I didn't mean to."

And then I found myself reaching out to her, gathering Lucy in my own arms, and hugging her close to my chest. My little sister rested her head on my shoulder and cried onto my shirt. I hugged her tighter and reached up to stroke her red hair.

"It'll be alright, Lucy," I said.

"Dad'll kill me."

"No he won't."

"He will. I *know* he will."

For probably the first time in my life I was torn and didn't know what to do. I was only nine and couldn't decide between telling Dad, or protecting my little sister. Lucy had killed Boots, but it wasn't like she'd killed a person. Boots was a kitten. Lucy was my little sister and she was only seven. It wasn't like she'd meant to kill the kitten. At least that's what I thought then.

"I'll fix it, Lucy."

Lucy squeezed me tightly and cried some more. I hugged her to me and stroked her hair for a while. Then I gently pushed her away.

"Listen. Wipe your eyes. Go inside. Have a nice hot bath."

Lucy nodded and wiped her eyes with the back of her hands. She started to go, but stopped at the corner of the garage, and turned back.

"You won't tell Dad, will you, Mickey?"

I shook my head.

"Promise. Cross your heart and hope to die."

"I promise." I crossed my right hand over the left side of my chest. "Cross my heart and hope to die."

Lucy smiled. And then she was gone.

I followed her inside a few minutes later. I grabbed a bin liner from the kitchen and took it back outside. Behind the garage I put the dead kitten in the plastic bag, twisted the top tight, and looked for a place to hide it until later.

After Dad had got home and we'd eaten tea, I retrieved the bag and went out on my bike. I cycled down to the river Mersey, added a few rocks to the bin liner, tied a knot in the top of the bag, and hurled it as far out into the river as I could. There was a large splash and the bin liner disappeared from sight.

Goodbye Boots, I thought.

Dad got into quite a panic later when Boots was nowhere to be seen. He spent half an hour trying to call her in. The same again the next day and the next. After a few days though he gave up.

If Lucy had found herself in trouble I'd decided I'd take the blame for it but Dad didn't blame anybody.

Siblings

You know I haven't thought about the kitten incident for a long time. Not since the last time Lucy called asking her big brother to come and fix it for her. That must've been about eighteen months ago. Lucy was living in Northampton then. Now she lived in Derby.

After I'd showered and changed, I checked my address book and made a note of Lucy's address. I'd never visited her in Derby. Lucy and I just exchanged birthday and Christmas cards these days, but that was about it. It hadn't always been that way, Lucy and I had remained close for a while as adults but that changed the first time she called and asked her big brother to come and fix it.

This has to stop, Lucy. I thought. *It has to stop.*

Every time I went and fixed things for Lucy – and this would be the fifth time – I told her it had to stop. Usually when I was hugging her close and stroking her hair. Lucy would be crying into my shoulder and between her tears she would agree to stop it.

"I'm sorry, Mickey. I'll stop. This will be the last time. I will stop. I promise. Cross my heart and hope to die."

And each and every time I really think Lucy meant it.

But, in the end, she couldn't help herself.

This has to stop, Lucy.

I always had a bag of gear ready for when she called needing her big brother. I kept it in the cupboard under the stairs. On the way out of the house, I grabbed the Lucy bag, locked the front door, and got into my car. After programming Lucy's post code into the Sat Nav, I backed off the drive and began my journey to Derby.

Dad's drinking got worse after the kitten incident. He never got violent – at least not with Lucy or me – but we heard he got into a few scrapes down the local pub. He did have a temper though and he'd fly off the handle at the least thing. Both of us kept a low profile when he'd been drinking and we went out of our way not to annoy or antagonise him.

When I escaped to Aston University that left Lucy at home with Dad. She would have been seventeen going on eighteen. I remember because she was having driving lessons and refused point blank to let Dad take her out in the car. Dad wanted to, and he offered all the time from what Lucy told me later, but she had none of it.

"He's a drunk, Mickey," she told me once. "And I won't be getting in the car with a drunk – even though I'm the one behind the wheel."

"Dad's that bad?" I'd asked.

"He drinks a lot, Mickey," she went on. "Much more than when you were here. And while things are okay, Mickey, they're not great. He hasn't laid a finger on me but his mood swings are worse than ever and I live in fear of him losing his temper and doing something bad."

I offered to come home, but Lucy told me to get on with my life and not worry. "Get your degree, Mickey." I asked if there was anything I could do, but Lucy told me she was handling it and she'd call if she needed help.

So just as Lucy had been on her own when she found Mum dead at the bottom of the stairs, my little sister was once again on her own when Dad died.

I regret that too.

In the end, it was the drink that killed Dad. Lucy called me from home and there were no tears. I remember that quite distinctly. No tears, just a matter-of-fact explanation.

"Dad had been drinking, Mickey," Lucy told me. "No surprise there. And he was driving home from wherever he'd been. Some pub or another. Anyway he was going down Oakfield Road."

"Uh-huh."

"And the junction with Stockport Road."

"Yeah," I said. "I know the one."

"He was involved in a head-on collision. Must've been going at some speed too."

"Oh my God."

"But that's not all. He wasn't wearing a seat belt so he crashed through the windscreen."

"Jesus." I closed my eyes and imagined the scene. Dad's crumpled car. Dad sprawled across the bonnet. Glass and blood everywhere. It didn't take much imagination as I'd seen enough road traffic accidents during my career.

"The police told me he was dead when they got there."

"I guess he would be. How was the other driver?"

"Just minor injuries."

"That's something."

"Dad was way over …" She started crying. "Over … the … drink … drive … limit."

"Are you okay, Lucy?"

"Yes … No … Yes … I don't know."

"I'll be there," I said.

So I went home and between us we sorted the death certificate, the funeral, the probate, all Dad's accounts, and the insurances. Well, almost on our own, Mr and Mrs Hitchcock from next door, or Kevin and Gillian as we now called them, were a great help. In fact, thinking about it now, they did most of the work, Lucy and I just did the running around. I'm not sure either of us would have got through it without Kevin and Gillian's support.

We talked about the house and stuff. We agreed to pay off the mortgage with the insurance money and split the rest between us. Any other money Dad had in the bank we also split equally. After a lengthy and at times heated debate, we decided to keep the house for Lucy to live in while she completed her 'A' levels at school and for as long as we needed it as the *family* home after that. If Lucy went to University (as she said she wanted to – "If it's good enough for my big brother, then it's good enough for me.") then we'd sell it and split the proceeds. If not, well we'd cross that bridge when we came to it.

My University year was coming to an end so I didn't go back. I stayed through some of the summer holidays. All told I probably stayed a couple of months, long enough to get Dad's affairs in order and for the insurance companies to agree to pay up.

Lucy and I remained close, but it wasn't the same as when we were kids. I hadn't realised it but I'd grown up a lot since leaving for University and Lucy was still a kid. We got on well when we talked, and shared a beer or two or three, but we didn't seem to have much in common any more. That summer we didn't do a great deal together and that surprised me. Lucy had her own friends and her own life and I didn't fit in. Besides, I spent a lot of my time down the town library, or pouring over my books at home, trying to keep up with my Biology studies.

In the end it was Lucy who told me to go back to my University digs. "It's been great having you stay," she said. "But you need to get on with your life."

"Will you be, okay?"

"Yeah, Mickey. I'll be fine. And if I'm not, I'll give you a call."

"Okay."

I don't know if it was coincidence or not but she sent me packing about a week after I found out she fancied girls.

I'd been out for most of the day although I can't remember what I'd been doing. I don't think I'd been down the library because University had finished for the year, but I may have been going through some of the biology books trying to get a head start ready for the new year. But I think it's more likely I'd been hanging out with some of my old friends from school.

Either way, I got home late in the afternoon and felt pretty hungry. I called out for Lucy, intending to see if she wanted something to eat too, but there was no reply. I couldn't find her downstairs so I started up the stairs, calling her name. Music was coming from her bedroom so I tapped three times on the door, as I always did, and went in.

"Lucy, do you—" The rest of the question remained unasked as I stared, mouth wide open, at Lucy's bed. She lay on her side underneath crumpled covers, her red hair fanned out on the pillow. Lying next to her, arms around her, kissing her, was a blonde girl.

"Get out!" Lucy hollered. She sat up and the covers fell away revealing my sister's breasts. "Get out!" she shouted again and threw a pillow at me.

"Sorry," I said, and backed out the room.

As I retreated down the stairs I heard them laughing but I guess that kind of spoilt the mood for them as Lucy's *friend* – Caroline, her name was – left not much more than half an hour later. Fully clothed, the blonde gave me a cheeky smile and a wave goodbye as she walked past me on her way out.

"Don't you *ever* do that again!" Lucy said once Caroline had gone.

"I'm sorry. I didn't know."

"That's not the point. Don't barge into my room like that again."

"Okay. It won't happen again."

"Make sure it doesn't."

And that was that. We didn't talk any more about it. Lucy said she was hungry so I went out to get some fish and chips. By the time I got back she had calmed down and things were back to normal. Or as normal as they ever got between us as adults. We curled up on the sofa and watched a couple of videos Lucy had rented earlier that day. We laughed and joked and, all in all, it was a good evening.

I knew Lucy had had boyfriends before, and from the conversations we'd had and the condoms I found in her handbag once when helping her find a set of keys she'd lost, I knew she wasn't a virgin, so finding her in bed with a girl was more of a surprise than a shock.

I asked her about it once and she said, "I'm not gay, Mickey. I'm not a lesbian, if that's what you're thinking. I just like girls as well as boys."

I nodded non-committally and said it was none of my business.

"The thing is though. I don't care about the boys. With the boys it's just sex. And it's fun. But with the girls it's different. The sex is different because girls intuitively know what turns another girl on but there's one obvious drawback. But I care about the girls more. That's the thing. I don't care about the boys but I do care about the girls. Does that make me a lesbian, Mickey?"

"I don't know. It's none of my business."

"Mickey?"

"It's none of my business."

"Does it?"

I sighed and she tilted her head to one side in the way she had when she wanted me to open the cardboard box containing the kitten.

"Do you really want my opinion?"

"Yes, Mickey."

"Well," I was still thinking what to say and did not make eye contact. "If you're asking me then, to be perfectly honest, I think it means you're *both* straight and gay." I looked up and Lucy was smiling at me. "There's a word for it. Now what is it?"

"Bi," Lucy said. "Bi-sexual."

"Yeah," I nodded. "I think you're bi-sexual."

"Good. That's what I think too." Lucy came over and sat next to me on the sofa.

"Does it bother you?"

I looked at her. Looked at her red hair, her big brown eyes, and the worried expression on her face.

"It doesn't bother me," I said. "I just want you to be happy."

And with that her face lit up and she threw her arms around me. I hugged her back.

That was later though and, like I said, it was about a week after I'd walked in on Lucy and her girlfriend in bed together that she told me to go and get on with my life.

So I did. I went back to Birmingham and continued studying for my Biology degree at Aston University. I'd tried out for the University football team in my first year and made the reserve squad. This time when I tried out I made the first team. I also got myself a job as a waiter in one of the local restaurants.

With my studies, job, plus football training and matches there wasn't time for anything else. I didn't give Lucy much thought to be honest. We spoke on the telephone a few times – usually when she called me – and exchanged the odd letter. Lucy wrote me, more than I wrote her.

But, to be honest, we didn't seem to connect as adults in a way we'd connected when we were growing up. As kids we had a lot of fun together and, at times, were inseparable. We were always laughing and joking and I still remember the way my little sister laughed, throwing back her head, her red hair flying through the air. But now, as adults, we had little in common. We had our own lives, we did our own thing, and we hardly ever laughed. Somehow, living with Dad on her own for eighteen months or so, Lucy had changed into a very serious and insular person.

We decided it would be good to spend that first Christmas together after Dad died. So I went home.

I wouldn't say we had a Merry Christmas, or even a good Christmas, but we did have an okay time. We exchanged presents but they were joke, novelty presents really. Lucy didn't buy me anything I wanted or needed and I don't think she ever found a use for the things I bought for her.

Somehow Lucy and I had gone from being inseparable to being unable to connect with each other at all.

Lucy used to be the chatterbox of the family and getting her to shut up was the problem. Now, it seemed sometimes, getting her to say more than a couple of sentences was the problem. And there were times when

Lucy just didn't hear me at all. I'd say something, or ask her something, and there'd be no response, like she was looking inside herself, lost in her own thoughts.

This time it was me who suggested I should return to Birmingham earlier than originally planned. Lucy protested, but there was no conviction to it.

So I went back to Birmingham and we got on with our lives. We kept in touch but the phone calls became less frequent and the letters became shorter, particularly the ones I wrote.

I made the offer to return home for Christmas again the following year but Lucy was busy and had other plans – I think she was going to Scotland with Caroline and some friends of theirs. To be honest, that came as a relief.

We got on with our lives.

Football and University continued to be my life and both went well. I became a regular starter up front for the University first team and was the top goal scorer every season until I graduated with a 2.1 degree in Biology and an offer to play semi-professional for Willenhall Town.

I found myself a job in the Police and made good progress there. I started off as a PC, walking the beat, being the first on the scene at road traffic accidents and scenes of crime. And yes, before you ask, I did throw up when I saw my first dead body or, to be more precise, my first *decomposing* dead corpse. Don't believe what they say though, trust me, it's not the sight of the dead body that makes you nauseas, it's the smell. It gets into the very mucous of your nose, making you gag, and it stays there a long time.

My interest in biology meant I was always getting into anatomical discussions and debates with the scene of crime officers, not to mention my colleagues and superiors at briefings. I was forever finding clues and suggesting areas to follow up based on the positioning of a victim and this saw me progress rapidly onto the investigative teams. For me, though, the appeal was the science of a crime, not the investigation of it. I was encouraged to study further. I did. And once fully qualified I became a scene of crime officer myself.

Every October or November I suggested to Lucy that we should get together for Christmas and every year, without fail, she had something planned. So another year would pass without us seeing each other.

Lucy's 'A' level grades were more than enough to secure her place at University, but she opted to take a job as a Customer Service Assistant with a Building Society instead.

She did well for herself too. After six months or so she transferred from the small branch in Altrincham to a larger branch in Sale. Within a couple of years she became a Management Trainee, and a year after that she gained promotion to Assistant Manager at the Stockport branch.

Lucy was doing well for herself. I was proud of her and expected her to be writing me to say she was managing her own branch in the not too distant future but, instead, she rang to ask her big brother to come and fix it for her.

I remember that call like it was yesterday, although it must've been just short of twenty years ago. I answered the phone and thought *this is it, Lucy's been promoted to branch manager*.

"Mickey? Is that you?" As soon as I heard the fear in her voice I knew this wasn't going to be a good news call.

"Yeah, Lucy." I said. "What's up?"

And Lucy burst into tears. She must've cried for the best part of two minutes before I could make out any words at all. And even then the words were garbled, random, and made no sense.

"Lucy," I said. "Calm down. Take a deep breath. And another. Now, tell me, what's up?"

"Oh, Mickey, I'm so sorry ..."

"About what?"

There was a long pause then. I didn't break the silence, just listened to my little sister's deep breaths and false starts on the other end of the telephone.

"Take your time, Lucy. I'm here for you."

"Are you, Mickey? Are you really?"

"Of course, I am."

"No matter what?"

"No matter what." I confirmed. And there and then, without realising it, my fate and my destiny were sealed.

"Do you remember, Boots?"

"Yeah," I said. In truth I hadn't thought about the kitten in a long time. I think I'd buried the bin liner containing the dead kitten deep in the recesses of my memory and chained it down there, out of sight. Now the memories came flooding back: a much younger Lucy, standing with her arms out straight, tightly holding the kitten by its neck, squeezing it, throttling it, strangling the life out of it.

"I thought we agreed never to talk about that."

"We did ... but–"

"What's going on, Lucy?"

"Did you mean what you just said, Mickey?"

"Mean what?"

"That you were here for me? No matter what?"

"Yes. Of course, I did."

"Do you promise? Cross your heart and hope to die?"

"I promise. Cross my heart and hope to die."

"Good," Lucy said and let out a long sigh. "You remember when I … when Boots … died. You remember how you fixed it for me?"

"I remember." Of course, I remembered.

"I'm sorry … I'm so sorry … I didn't mean to … I really didn't mean to … but I need you to fix it for me again. Will you come fix it for me, Mickey?"

"Fix what, Lucy?"

She was sobbing again and I could get nothing that made any sense out of her other than her repeated pleas of, "Will you come, Mickey? Will you fix it?"

There really wasn't a question to answer. Lucy was my little sister and I loved her deeply, even if our relationship had become strained and difficult in a way I didn't understand. I would always be there for her.

Always.

So I went.

I fixed it.

Oh, Lucy. This has to stop.

And after I fixed it, we grew even further apart.

There were no more telephone calls, but there were still letters. Lucy continued to write, albeit less frequently, but I no longer replied to every letter. After two or three letters piled up though, I'd feel guilty, and I'd make myself sit down and write my little sister.

Lucy couldn't settle. She got herself a transfer to the Wigan branch, which meant we finally had to sell the house so that she could relocate. Lucy handled the sale through the Building Society's Estate Agent contacts. To be fair, we got a very good sale price.

We split the proceeds between us.

Whatever problems Lucy had, moving to Wigan didn't solve them. Nine months later she transferred branches and moved house again. A recurring pattern was set and every six to twelve months she'd get another transfer and move house again. At first staying as Assistant Manager but after a few moves she went back to being a Customer Service Assistant again.

Looking back, I wish I'd done more to help Lucy.

But by then I'd moved house myself. I was living in Enfield and working with the Metropolitan Police as part of the largest Forensics Team in the country.

And I'd also met Jenny – who would go on to become my wife, and later my ex-wife – and I didn't want Lucy, and whatever crazy madness was going on with my little sister, getting in the way of my relationship with Jenny.

So I left Lucy to deal with her problems alone.

That's another regret.

Just as she'd had to find Mum dead at the bottom of the stairs herself; just as she'd had to deal with the aftermath of Dad's drinking and his fatal car crash by herself.

Lucy unravelled by herself and I let it happen.

More regrets.

And, of course, Lucy did come between Jenny and me.

Jenny could never understand why every time Lucy rang I had to drop everything and go visit her as a matter of urgency.

Oh no, Lucy. Not again.

And let's be honest here, I really couldn't blame Jenny. After all, we were talking about a sister Jenny had never met; a sister she'd never even seen a photograph of; a sister who I refused to invite to our wedding. Yet whenever my sister called, I packed a bag and went to see her.

Oh no, Lucy. This has to stop.

I couldn't blame Jenny for not understanding. Hell, I'm not sure I even understood myself. But the thing I think that hurt Jenny the most was that I never attempted to explain it to her.

"Why, Mike? Tell me why. Why do you have to go?"

"I just have to."

"Why?"

"Because she's my sister."

"Your sister. You could've fooled me. You don't act like siblings. You have nothing to do with each other for years and years and then out of the blue she rings and you go to her."

"I don't want to talk about it."

"Why not? What are you hiding?"

"Nothing."

"Then why can't you tell me?"

"I don't want to talk about it."

Yeah, reliving the numerous conversations we had like that, I can't blame Jenny at all.

But it would also be unfair to blame the failure of my marriage on my sister. It wasn't Lucy who drove the wedge between my ex-wife and me. Oh, no. I took a great big sledgehammer to that wedge and drove it all the way in myself. I don't even blame Jenny. I did at the time, but not now. Not one bit.

It wasn't even work, although that was a major contributing factor. I worked long hours, and I worked irregular hours, and I could be called out at any time. Day or night. Usually at the most inappropriate times – during a romantic meal, when we were at the theatre or the cinema, when we were making love.

And there, I think, we had the crux of the problem. We made love, but we didn't make love enough. Certainly not enough for Jenny. And definitely not enough to get Jenny pregnant. That was another thing I couldn't talk to her about, even though Jenny was desperate to have children. I don't know what the problem was. It could've simply been the accumulated angst and stress in our relationship, or there could've been a medical problem, but we never got around to finding out.

Oh, no. I drove that wedge between us all by myself.

I'm surprised our marriage lasted as long as it did to be honest. I came home from work one day and my wife was gone. There was a hand written note on my pillow that read, "Dear Mike, All I ever wanted was to be happy and I'm not happy. I haven't been happy for a long time. I can't do this any more. I think we will both be happier if we go our separate ways. I want a divorce. Jenny."

I couldn't argue with that. I let Jenny go and I didn't contest the divorce.

Jenny didn't deserve to be treated the way I treated her.

And that's why I've been ignoring Stacey's messages because I don't trust myself. Stacey deserves better than to have a wedge driven between us somewhere down the line.

But it's Lucy I need to focus on to complete my confession. As soon as I heard my little sister's message I knew what I was going to find.

"Mickey, it's happened again. I'm so sorry. You're my big brother and I need you to fix it. Will you come fix it?"

I knew because it had happened four times before. Five if you included Boots the kitten.

Oh, Lucy. This has to stop.

When Sat Nav told me I'd reached my destination I kept driving and turned left. I made a couple more turns and parked by the side of the road. It was dark by now but I was taking no chances.

I grabbed the Lucy bag, got out of the car, locked it, and headed back towards Lucy's place.

At the end of her road I stopped, and looked carefully in all directions. Satisfied nobody was about, I reached inside the Lucy bag and took out a pair of disposable gloves. I checked all around me again. All clear. I put on the gloves and walked briskly down the road.

When I reached the bottom of Lucy's drive, I checked one more time that nobody was about.

I took a pair of disposable shoe covers out of the Lucy bag, and walked up the drive to the front door. Here I set the bag down on the *W*E*L*C*O*M*E* mat and slipped the covers over my shoes. Picking up the bag, I pressed the door bell once and heard it ring inside the house.

Soon enough the sound of shuffling feet came down the hallway and I saw Lucy's silhouette through the dimpled glass in the door. The sound of a key turning in the lock, a bolt pulled back, a chain unhooked, and the front door opened.

Lucy looked worse than I'd ever seen her and, remember, she'd called me to fix it four times before. Her face looked tired and old, her eyes were bloodshot, her cheeks were stained with mascara tracks, her hair hung lank and greasy. She wore a fluffy white dressing gown that she'd belted tightly around the waist.

A sad excuse for a smile touched her lips briefly, so brief I wasn't sure I'd actually seen it, and then she turned her back and walked down the hallway.

Stepping inside the house, I closed the door behind me, turned the key, drew the bolt, and fixed the chain.

"Lucy?" I called out.

"In here," a soft, quivering voice.

I followed the voice into the living room and found exactly what I'd expected to find. A dead girl lying on the rug in front of the gas fire, a kitchen knife lodged in her throat; blood on her neck, down her front, over the mounds of her breasts, and on her bra, stomach and panties. There was blood on her hands, fingers and arms which suggested she hadn't died straight away. More blood covered the rug.

"Oh, Lucy," I said. "Not again."

"I'm sorry," she said softly. "I didn't mean to. I *loved* her."

I looked over and Lucy was curled up on the sofa, her legs tucked underneath her. There were tears running down her face.

"You never mean to."

"I know. I'm so sorry."

I nodded and took a couple of steps towards the dead girl. I looked more closely, taking in the details. Everything seemed the same as the previous times I'd fixed it. Say one thing about Lucy she was consistent. Her modus operandi never changed. Always a girl, never a boy. The only thing that changed was the colour of the victim's hair and what she had been wearing. This girl was blonde, making her the second blonde. There'd also been a brunette and a girl with long black hair.

I set my bag down on the floor and without looking back at Lucy, I said, "This has to stop."

"I know."

"I mean it, Lucy. This has to be the last time."

"I do want it to stop."

I bent down and pulled the disposable overalls out of the bag. I started to put them on.

"Mickey?"

"Yes," I turned round. She was staring at me with those big brown eyes of hers and she looked so sad. Tears continued to streak her face with mascara tracks."

"I want you to make it stop, Mickey."

"I can't, Lucy. You have to stop this."

She sobbed then. There was something different about Lucy this time that I couldn't quite put my finger on. I wanted to go over and hug her, to comfort her, but I didn't. I put the overalls on.

When she'd composed herself a little, Lucy said, "I can't stop it, Mickey. I've tried. I've tried so hard, but I can't stop."

"I know." There were tears in my eyes now.

"I need *you* to make it stop. Will you stop it, Mickey?"

I nodded and felt the first tear tracks on my own cheeks.

"Will you end it?"

I nodded.

"Say it."

"Yes. I'll end it."

"Promise? Cross your heart and hope to die?"

"Yes." I crossed my heart with my right hand. "Cross my heart and hope to die."

Lucy smiled then and, for a brief moment, her face lit up and I saw the young Lucy that I'd had so many happy times with growing up once again. Then the smile was gone.

"Go run yourself a nice hot bubble bath," I said. "I'll find you when I'm done."

Lucy didn't say anything. She slid her legs out from underneath her and got to her feet. The dressing gown had loosened and I could tell she wore nothing underneath. She took a few steps towards the door then paused and looked over at me, a puzzled expression adding lines to her face.

"Lucy."

And there was that wonderful smile again. She walked over to me and gently planted a kiss on my cheek. "Thank you for being my big brother."

She stepped back and the smile was gone. She turned and walked away.

I listened and waited. I listened to her footsteps going up the stairs. I listened to the sound of water running into the bath. I waited for the water to stop running. I waited for the sound of her getting into the bath.

Then I turned my attention back to the dead girl.

Oh, Lucy, I thought. *This has to stop*.

As I prepared to get to work, I kept thinking about Lucy's demeanour since I'd arrived. She seemed sadder and more remorseful than I'd seen her before. This was closer to the first time I'd fixed it for her – not Boots the kitten, but the first time she'd killed a person – because she didn't know I *would* fix it. The second, third, and fourth times there was a kind of confidence to her demeanour because she *knew* I'd fix it for her. This time was more like that first time but there was a deeper sadness to it. As I took the cleaning materials out of the bag, I went over the conversation we'd just had in my mind.

"I can't stop it, Mickey. I've tried. I've tried so hard, but I can't stop."

"I know."

"I need *you* to make it stop. Will you stop it, Mickey?"
I'd nodded.

"Will you end it?"
I'd nodded again.

"Say it."

"Yes. I'll end it."

And then Lucy had done that thing she'd done ever since we were little kids playing in the garden together. She'd made me promise and cross my heart and hope to die.

Oh, Lucy, I thought. *Do you really want me to make it stop? Do you really want me to end it?*

I stood up, walked into the hallway, and climbed the stairs. I'd never been to Lucy's place in Derby before and had no idea where the bathroom was.

At the top of the stairs I looked around. There were five doors. Four of them were closed; the other wide open.

I went towards the open door and saw a sink and toilet. I walked through the door and found Lucy in the bath. She was lying full length and there were plenty of bubbles to hide her modesty. Her head tilted back, resting on a flannel on the edge of the bath. Her eyes were closed and all the mascara stains had been washed away. She looked so relaxed and peaceful that, for a while, I just stood there staring at her.

"That was fast," she said without opening her eyes.

"I haven't fixed it yet. Do you want me to?"

She opened her big, brown eyes and stared at me. We stayed like that for a long time. As kids we'd often play the staring game; staring into each other's eyes and the one who blinked first lost. This was something like that but it wasn't a game. I think we were both weighing each other up, hoping we were once again on the same wavelength.

"No," Lucy said finally. "I don't want you to fix it."

I knelt by the side of the bath and reached into the water with a gloved hand. I gathered some bubbles on my fingers and tickled her nose with them. She closed her eyes and smiled.

"Do you want me to stop it?"

"Yes, Mickey."

"To end it?"

"Yes."

"Are you sure?"

"Absolutely." Lucy opened her eyes and there were tears in them. "I love you, Mickey."

I kissed the second and third fingers of my gloved right-hand and then placed them on my little sister's lips.

"I wish you didn't have to wear those."

"Me too," I said.

"I'm ready," Lucy said and closed her eyes.

"Just relax," I said, stroking her damp hair with my right hand. "Keep your eyes closed, relax, and go to sleep."

With my right hand I continued to stroke her hair and with my left hand I cleared the bubbles away, pushing them further down the bath. As the water cleared I got a good view of Lucy's breasts and nipples. I looked away and gazed at my little sister's calm and peaceful face.

I don't know how long I knelt there, stroking her hair, listening to her breathing, watching the gentle rise and fall of her chest. I totally lost track of time. It might have been thirty seconds, or it might have been thirty minutes. However long it was, I finally decided it was long enough.

My right hand stopped stroking Lucy's hair and gently slid under the back of her head. I placed my left hand firmly between her breasts.

"I love you, Lucy," I said.

Gently, almost tenderly, I pushed down on her chest with my left hand and eased her head into the water with my right. I watched as first her chin, then her mouth, then her nose, forehead, and hair disappeared under the water. I wasn't using anywhere near my full force and waited for any sign of resistance or struggle but there wasn't any.

Little bubbles escaped from her nose and mouth and rose to the surface. I continued to push down gently on her chest and her forehead, all the time expecting her to fight against me and sit up, gasping for breath.

I'd already decided that this was a one time deal. That at the first sign of a struggle or resistance I'd let Lucy surface, catch her breath, and then go downstairs and fix it as I'd fixed it before.

But there was no struggle or resistance. As I continued pushing her head down to the bottom of the bath, her hair floated upwards, fanning out.

I watched the small bubbles floating to the surface as she took her final breaths. She looked beautiful, and relaxed, and she was smiling.

And then Lucy pushed against me. A flurry of bubbles escaped to the surface. Her head rose and she struggled to gain purchase with her hands. Her forehead broke the surface and I pushed down hard with both hands, one on her forehead, one on her face.

I know I'd planned to let her up at the first sign of trouble ... but I didn't. I pushed down with everything I had. The truth was I wanted this to stop.

I *needed* it to stop.

Lucy continued to struggle. She reached up and grabbed my hands. She was strong, but her strength was waning.

"Calm down," I said. Not knowing whether she could hear me. The bubbles from her nose and mouth the only response. "Calm down, Lucy. It'll be over soon."

Her big brown eyes opened wide underneath the water and stared at me. I closed my own eyes – I couldn't bear the eye contact – and pushed down with everything I had. My arms ached with the effort.

She struggled for a while but soon her arms fell away and her head no longer fought against my hands.

I opened my eyes and looked into the water. Lucy's eyes had closed.

The frequency between the bubbles grew longer and longer until there were no bubbles at all. Even then, just when I thought she was gone, another bubble would escape and float to the surface.

Finally, after what seemed an eternity, there were no more bubbles.

"Goodbye, Lucy," I said. "Rest in peace."

I took my time after that. I gathered all my gear together, put it in the Lucy bag, and placed it by the front door. Then I checked each room before I left, even those I hadn't been in. I checked the living room and the bathroom thoroughly and meticulously. Back at the front door I removed the disposable overalls and put them in the bag.

"I love you, Lucy," I said and went through the door.

I kept the disposable gloves and shoe covers on until I got to the bottom of the road. Then I removed them, put them in the Lucy bag, and hurried to my car. The bag went in the boot.

Once inside the car I opened the glove compartment and took out the tape recorder. I inserted a brand new tape.

I didn't start recording this confession straight away. It would take a couple of hours to drive from Derby to Enfield so I waited until I'd cleared Derby and reached the M1.

Then I pressed record and began this confession.

You know I often wonder why Lucy started killing when she did. I guess it all started with Boots the kitten … but I'm not sure it really did start then. I think the kitten was more an accident than anything else. I think Lucy was frustrated and angry with the kitten and she just grabbed it by the neck. I don't think Lucy was aware of her own strength. I don't think she meant to kill the kitten.

No, I think it really started when she killed the first girl. Whether she meant to kill her, or any of the others, I don't know … but kill them she did.

I wonder about whether or not it was a coincidence that I was already a scene of crime officer by the time of the first killing? Did that factor into Lucy's thinking at any point or was it mere coincidence? In fiction coincidences are hard to take seriously but in real life, especially when investigating crimes, I've found coincidences happen all the time.

But what I wonder about the most is this: *If I hadn't joined the police, if I hadn't become a scene of crime officer, would those girls still be alive?*

I wonder about that a lot and it does keep me awake at night.

For the record, and this tape, I've already mentioned Lucy's first victim. Caroline Jackson. She was the blonde girl I found Lucy in bed with that time.

This last victim, according to her credit cards, was Harriet Miles. I've left all her ID in Lucy's flat for when someone finds them.

I can't remember the names of Lucy's other victims but I still have their IDs hidden away at home. When I'm done, I'll put this tape, together with all the IDs and a note of how and where I disposed of the bodies, in a jiffy bag and store it in the safety deposit box I hold with the bank.

After that, well I'll wait and see how things go.

But I won't forget about Lucy and her victims and the role I played in all that. I will make this confession known at some point but now is not the time to decide how and when.

If I start getting serious heat when Harriet and my little sister's bodies are found, and I mean *serious* heat, not just standard procedure heat, then I'll come clean.

If not, then I'm going to make a real, belated attempt to live and lead a normal life. If I'm able to make a go of that then I'll make provisions to ensure the jiffy bag is found after my death.

I guess though, after everything you've heard about my life so far, you'll agree the odds are heavily stacked against me being able to live and lead a normal life. In which case I won't draw out the agony the families of Lucy's victims have suffered any longer than needs be.

This ends my confession.

Please don't think too badly of me.

I have plans now and I'm going to do my best to live and lead a normal life.

I'm close to Enfield and nearly home. I'll just have time for a quick shower, and change of clothes, before driving to the mortuary for the post-mortems.

When I finish work I'll give Stacey a ring, apologise profusely, and see if she wants to see me again. I think we could have something Stacey and I.

I hope I get the opportunity to find out.

Biographies

Richard Farren Barber was born in Nottingham in July 1970. After studying in London he returned to the East Midlands. He lives with his wife and son and works as a Development Services Manager for a local university.

He has had short stories published in *Alt-Dead*, *Alt Zombie*, *Blood Oranges*, *Derby Scribes Anthology*, *ePocalypse – Tales from the End*, *The Horror Zine*, *Murky Depths*, *Midnight Echo*, *Midnight Street*, *Morpheus Tales*, *MT Urban Horror Special*, *Night Terrors II*, *The House of Horror*, *Trembles*, *Terror Scribes* and broadcast on *BBC Radio Derby and Erewash Sound*.

During 2010/11 Richard was sponsored by *Writing East Midlands* to undertake a mentoring scheme in which he was supported in the development of his novel *Bloodie Bones*, which he is now shamelessly hawking amongst agents and publishers.

His website is www.richardfarrenbarber.co.uk

Sam Stone is the award-winning author of *The Vampire Gene* Series and the horror collection *Zombies in New York and Other Bloody Jottings*. Her latest works include the fifth vampire gene novel *Silent Sand* and *Zombies At Tiffany's* : a Steampunk/horror novella.

She lives in North Wales in a vampire lair under Rhuddlan Castle with her partner David, her daughter Linzi, and an aged Renfield with a lisp and a hunch.

Sara Jayne Townsend was born in Cheshire in 1969 and spent most of the 1980s in Canada when her family emigrated there. She has two novels, *Suffer the Children* and *Death Scene*, published as e-books by Lyrical Press, and available from most e-book retailers. Her latest publication is *Soul Screams* by Stumar Press. She is founder and Chair of the T Party Writers' Group, and currently lives in Surrey with her guitarist husband and two elderly cats.

Her website is sarajaynetownsend.weebly.com

Simon Kurt Unsworth was born in Manchester in 1972 on a night when, despite increasingly desperate research, he can find no evidence of mysterious signs or portents. He currently lives on a hill in the north of England with his wife and child awaiting the coming flood, where he writes essentially grumpy fiction (for which pursuit he was nominated for a 2008 World Fantasy Award for Best Short Story) whilst being tall, grouchier than he should be and owning a wide selection of garish shirts. His latest collection is the critically acclaimed *Quiet Houses*, and his work has been published in a number of anthologies including *At Ease with the Dead*, *Shades of Darkness*, *Exotic Gothic 3* and *Lovecraft Unbound*. He has also appeared in four *Mammoth Book of Best New Horror* anthologies and also *The Very Best of Best New Horror*. His first collection of short stories, *Lost Places*, was released by the Ash Tree Press in 2010 and he has further collections due, *Strange Gateways* from PS Publishing in 2012 and his as-yet-unnamed collection will launch the Spectral Press *Spectral Signature Editions* imprint in 2013, so at some point he needs to write those stories.

Stuart Hughes's last publication was *Busy Blood* (theEXAGGERATEDpress) - a collection of eleven short stories Stuart collaboratively wrote with D. F. Lewis. "Adroitly written tales of the fantastic for the discerning connoisseur. A wonderful synthesis of mysterious delights and freakish surprises - expect the unexpected!" - Simon Clark.

Stuart was born in Burton upon Trent in March 1965. He started writing seriously in 1988 and his first short story was published a year later. Since then he has had over 80 short story credits in various anthologies, magazines, newspapers, and broadcast on radio.

In 1997, eleven of his short stories were published in the collection *Ocean Eyes*. His second short story collection will be published by theEXAGGERATEDpress in 2013.

For nine years Stuart edited the award winning magazine *Peeping Tom*, which won the British Fantasy Award in 1991 and 1992. Stuart is a member of the British Fantasy Society and the writers group Derby Scribes. He is currently working on his first novel.

His website can be found at www.stuarthughes.webs.com and theEXAGGERATEDpress can be found at www.exaggeratedpress.weebly.com

Fogbound From 5, Alt-Dead, Alt-Zombie. Siblings

all © Hersham Horror Books 2012

Chapter Bank © Simon Kurt Unsworth 2012

Imogen © Sam Stone 2012

Skin Deep © Richard Farren Barber 2012

Always The Baby © Sara Jayne Townsend 2012

My Little Sister © Stuart Hughes 2012

Siblings

Coming 2013 from

Hersham Horror Books

THE ANTONOMY OF DEATH IN 5 SLEAZY PIECES

PentAnth No.3 Edited by Mark West

&

BITE SIZED HORROR 2

Edited by Johnny Mains

HTTP://HERSHAMHORRORBOOKS.WEBS.COM/